The Seventh Floor

By

Craig Leibfreid

Cover Art by Koa Beam

© Craig Leibfreid 2017

"God taught me how to forgive, and for that I am forever grateful"

    -Craig Leibfreid

"We do not inherit the Earth from are ancestors. We borrow it from our children."

    -Native American Proverb

CHAPTER 1

It was Friday, May 13th when James heard the sirens headed for his house. He knew who they were coming for, but James couldn't bring himself to evade the authorities and disappear into the woods. It was evil that brought him to this point. Every time he got close to that big red Dodge with the 'Hell Raiser' license plate his skin crawled, his stomach turned, and his brain boiled over with hatred so profane he could think of nothing but murdering the bastard who owned it. It was his father's truck.

James' father was a man's man. His name was Wade, and he had a cast-iron jaw, and brawny shoulders. He stood 6'4" tall and weighed somewhere between 225 and 240 pounds, depending on how much steak he ate, and how much beer he drank the night before. He wore a short black pony-tail, and rarely a shirt, and was always seen with a 16-ounce can of Genesee beer in hand. Wade knew what sacrifice meant. He made plenty of them to give James the life he had, but on James' 18th birthday, Wade sent him off to work in a slaughter house in Montana. It was James' turn to make sacrifices. Working in that butcher shop he spent long days covered in blood stabbing beef with his butcher knife. The hours of labor didn't bother him. The blood and smell of raw meat, though, he never got used to. Butchering his kill back home in the mountains of Appalachia was one thing. 11 hours of blood, and meat, and knife was something completely different. James kept up without complaining or showing remorse, but every man has his breaking point. And, young malleable minds snap louder than the patient, wise ones of old men. 5 years after arriving in Montana, he returned home. Home never seemed too antagonizing when James was a kid. Wade took him hunting and fishing, and his mother, Leah, always cooked and cleaned, taught him manners and made sure he did his homework. But, after spending those five years covered in blood something called to him, and demons chased him in his sleep. Every night he would wake up to adrenaline surging through his arms and hands with visions of blood soaked clothes and blood covered faces chasing him, crying "More, more, more." One day in early May, James couldn't take it any more, and he headed home

    When he got home, his parents could tell he wasn't the same man that left five long years ago. His mother was worried from the look in his eyes. He spent his many waking hours wide-eyed with an expression of detachment. He looked bothered and unsettled. He had something on his mind, but Leah couldn't empathize. She just worried and accused. Wade was too blunt and callous to see the trauma and delusions in James' mind. James was the work horse for a gluttonous demand. He metabolized in the underbelly of consumption, and after five long years of being covered in blood, his concept of reality was disgusted. After that much time, in those conditions, every waking hour was uncomfortable and disheveled. His emotions were a ball of hate and anger. His spirit yearned for purification, and cleansing, but all that his id could produce was revenge. He woke up one Friday morning, and as he walked past Wade's big red Dodge for the tenth time, he couldn't hold back his hatred anymore. Everything that haunted James in Montana blew back to him like a breeze blowing the pungent stench of hate in his face. He walked in the house, and grabbed the heaviest thing he could get out the door. Adrenaline exploded in his veins, and he furiously hurled it towards the the windshield of his father's pickup. As the 80 pound ceramic vat flew through the air, James felt emancipated, and time slowed down until it collided with the glass. The sound of the windshield shattering left James feeling hollow. As the 80 pound ceramic vat laid in the driver's seat, James couldn't believe what he had just done. He knew this wasn't the answer, and he wasn't even sure if destroying the truck's windshield would make him feel better, but he just wanted one person to feel the torment and destruction he had felt after those five years in the slaughter house.

James ran over the consequences in his head a couple of times, and as he played out the confrontation between himself and his father, it kept ending as one more bloody night with a knife in his hand. In fear of himself and in care of his father, James punched the numbers 9-1-1 into the touchtone phone. When the operator picked up all he could say was "Send the police."

James didn't know this, but that big red Dodge was an object of evil from the grill to the tailgate. When James walked past it, shivers ran up his spine as though the truck was trying to intimidate him. There was a subliminal animosity between James, and all the smooth transitions and brilliant colors of that big red Dodge. Volumes of evil were hidden in its clearcoat. Wade bought it used after James left for Montana, bought it cheap. The thing came from a police auction after some moonshiners in Appalachia were caught by the state troopers, but what no one knew was that that truck had been connected with kidnap, rape, and murder for near ten years. It hissed of evil, and stunk of evil, but James was the only one who could feel the devil's crippling wrath when they got near it. It was like a parasite festering with negative energy, and as James sat in the driveway looking at what he had done, the truck seemed to moan in pain. It seemed to resent James, and continued at its best to intimidate him with an icy embrace, and harsh frequencies. As it sat there with broken glass on the driver seat, the truck seemed to convulse in pain. It was as though the truck believed its saucy shell and brute strength was enough to seduce any man. But, before that Friday in early May, that truck never came face to face with James.

The police arrived at James' little mountain home. He never felt the urge to run until they began asking him questions. The fruition of his actions struck something in his consciousness. He knew he destroyed something beautiful, and now the consequences seemed real. James got up and began walking away. After ignoring the cop's commands to stop they took him down with a taser. They radioed for an ambulance, and when it arrived, the paramedics put James in a straight jacket, and bound him in the back of the meat wagon. He screamed and raged. They slammed the doors, turned on the sirens, and bolted for the hospital. Inside, James was a ball of fire. So much hate and fury was burning within, and no sensual stimulation could calm what he was feeling. An icy grip of evil had set him ablaze, and James wanted it all to burn down to the ground. He threw down the gauntlet. He finally hit his breaking point and couldn't take it anymore. He threw his punches, and was about to receive the blows of retaliation. He had no problem going to prison. He could handle the thugs and savagery of a penitentiary. But the hospital... he had no clue what he was in for.

When he arrived at the hospital, the paramedics wheeled James in, and they strapped him to a bed. He couldn't think of anything but how much he hated what his life had become. Nearly everyday for the past five years was spent with blood on his face and a knife in his hand. He'd walk the streets of Cut Bank, MT and see nothing but fat wallets and fat bellies. He was thrown face to face to the gripping reality that no matter how thick a person's wallet may be, there is no free lunch. He made the sacrifices to keep the masses fat and happy. Day in and day out he bathed in the liquid of life, and it gripped him in death. The stench of it all aroused senses he never knew he had, senses that pushed reason beyond nature down into the supernatural. Obscure energies jolted his subconscious. The stench was ingested, and the soul regurgitated an empty, hopeless anger. Blood coated the synapses in the body and mind until the nerves were dull and numb. As James worked the bodies down with his knife, an evil finesse crawled about his skin. Now all this spiritual antagonism had left him with nowhere to go. The straight jacket made him think about Montana and how he wished he would have just stayed out there. He left blood for hate. He didn't find hate; hate found him. It was brewing. James just laid in the bed and tried to recollect everything that brought him here; the blood covered days in Montana, and the big red Dodge in the driveway of his parents' house. What he couldn't fathom was what snapped inside of him when he decided to launch that 80 pound ceramic vat through the windshield of his father's truck. He was in somewhat of a destitute position. He had sunk into a sanguinary quicksand. He couldn't even bring himself to run and hide when he decided to call the cops on himself. No, instead he took a long ride in a straight jacket, in the back of a meat wagon, all the way to the hospital where doctors had to figure out what to do with him. He waited patiently just happy to be out of that straight jacket. He listened to the seconds tick by on the clock and bathed in the somber peace of each breath he took. Then his mother showed up.

"James, what the hell happened?" Leah asked. "You talked so badly of the past five years in Montana. I thought you were happy to be home, happy to see your father and I every morning when you wake up, and every night when you go to bed."

"I'm not the same man." James replied. "All I know is blood. There is something crawling inside of me that yearns for destruction. Everytime I walked past that truck my brain boiled. There's something evil about that truck, something disgusting, and it poked and prodded my soul until today , and I just couldn't take it anymore." He lost all rationale in an instant. His mother's eyes began to fill with tears as she sat beside her son. She was speechless and filled with the fear that some unspeakable transformation took place within James during those years he spent in Montana. He wasn't making sense to her. There was no physical representation of the things he was trying to explain to her. James was fighting phantoms, and to Leah those phantoms were nothing more than bits of his imagination. Still, she could see trouble and contempt in James' eyes. It pained and worried Leah to see her son in such a state. To her, James was letting his imagination get the best of him. To James, the goodness of his soul was being preyed upon by evil. It was something he couldn't explain. It was something bigger than him, but now he had no choice but address that something.

Chapter 2

James spent a few hours on the first floor of the hospital. Then after some of the doctors heard the conversation between him and his mother, they decided he was unfit to function in society. The doctors thought the only place for this nut was on the Seventh Floor, the psych-ward. They loosened the straps on the bed, put him in a wheel chair, and headed for an elevator. Along the way, James contemplated escaping. He knew he had it in him, but he felt so disheveled he didn't even bother to budge. He had nowhere to run and nowhere to hide. His mother had no clue what was going on inside of him, and she would never harbor James in the state he was in. He didn't have any close friends in town. Anyone who took one look at his face could tell he wasn't there. His mind was off in some far gory corner.

"Blood and a knife," James thought, "no man is meant to spend 70 hours a week covered in blood with a knife in his hand. Those bastards are sick. They're one bad day from spending a lifetime in prison. Even worse, they're one bad day away from killing someone. Blood is one fucking disgusting thing to get familiar with, to find comfort in. Maybe I should have gotten comfortable with it, then I wouldn't have high-tailed it home."

James was right. Blood is a disgusting thing the get comfortable with; the way it's warm and thin when the meat has been freshly killed, and turns cold and thick by the time you saw off the animal's head and legs. Though, it was the smell of the blood and raw flesh that made James so uncomfortable. Maybe he would have fared better if he just became comfortable with its familiarity, but what James didn't realize was how deep he saw into things. Blood was a mere symbol of pain being expelled from the body. Blood was a relationship of comfort within itself when a creature is living. Then, things are right, well, and good. After a quick laceration, comfort is broken as it pours from within. It oozed out with its red hue screaming at James "Feel me!" James felt it. Maybe he felt it more than any man should. The weight of its tyranny was bound to strike him sooner or later.

When James first arrived in Montana he had two weeks before he had to start working in the slaughter house. He was young, and eager to live, fresh out of the isolation of Appalachia. He moseyed around the streets of Cut Bank looking for anything to strike his fancy. He couldn't find it. There were women, and there was booze, but he was looking for something more transcending, more ideal, more intangible.

The culmination of everything symbolically significant to a people is their culture. Their art, their food, their religion is all an impression of who they are, and where and what they come from. Native Americans weren't completely driven off the land out west in the same way they were back east. James did a little investigating and learned the Blackfoot tribe was the original inhabitants of Cut Bank, MT. He came to find the Blackfoot natives captivating. Their religion and mysticism depicted such a way of life and a connection to the land that he could not turn his head and ignore them. Around camp fires along the edge of town, James met some Blackfoot Natives. They told stories of their people, and talked of a special place, Sweet Grass Hill. James was eager to learn about their culture. He asked to go to Sweet Grass Hill. He wanted to know what the Blackfoot knew. He asked to meet their chief, their medicine man, anyone who could enlighten him. James asked and the men turned him away. After a bit of drifting in the plains of north central Montana, James met a man who claimed to be half Crow, and half Blackfoot. His name was Paahsaakii, or Firefly. He was born the son of a Blackfoot woman, and a Crow father. Paahsaakii's mother brought him to Sweet Grass Hill when he was a child, but before long, the Blackfoot Chief learned of the woman's half-breed son, and banished them from the place. As Paahsaakii grew older, his father taught him the practice of the Peyote Medicine Rituals. Paahsaakii grew old and along the way, he served spiritual guidance for many souls turned away by their people. James was one of these people, a vagrant, a transient in search of his soul. James stood around a campfire in Ferdig, and a man with long grey hair and an elk skin robe stood across from him. This man knew many beliefs and practices of the Plains People. This man knew the power of Sweet Grass Hill. This man was Paahssaakii. Paahssaakii spoke slowly, and when James looked into his eyes James could see a man with great respect for the knowledge that he shared with James. Paahssaakii knew a great deal about the spirit of the Earth. He knew the culmination of energy and consciousness, and the power the two had when coupled together. The obscurities could be frightening, crippling even. It was out of sheer protection that these secrets were not shared with everyone, even to those who appear to respect what the spirit of the Earth may hold. There was a somber reverence in Paahssaakii's eyes and in his voice. The enlightenment James was searching for was a journey. Paahssaakii had taken that journey, but wanted to make sure that James understood that the path of enlightenment was not quick nor easy. After a couple hours together, James learned of a rite of passage by many tribes, a Vision Quest. It was said to be a connection of time and place, person and spirit. The Vision Quest was a feat to find direction in a young man's life. James wanted a vision to help direct his road. After their conversation they ventured to Sweet Grass Hill despite Paahsaakii's exile from the Blackfoot territory. Paahsaakii could see something in James, and he knew James would benefit greatly from such an experience. They spoke reservedly along the way.

"This is our place, and their place. This is where people meet the spirits that will guide them. You must be pure, and the spirits will come to you and guide you." Said Paahsaakii.

James wanted a vision quest and Paahsaakii gave James two options. The first was fasting for ten days. James didn't have that kind of self-control. He asked Paahsaakii what the second option was, and Paahsaakii held out his hand. In his palm was a little green cactus button of peyote. Paahsaakii explained the peyote would be more intense than fasting and the visions might be too confusing to understand. This option would open a world of feelings and ideas that would be hard to control and comprehend, but they would reveal the essence of everything that this world IS. Tastes, sights, sounds, and smells, would excite the feelings so powerfully that they would be capable of destroying a man's concept of reality in an effort to build a new one, one that is pure and righteous. It was a gamble, and James was about to roll the dice.

"Don't eat in the morning," Paahsaakii explained, "then we will walk to Sweet Grass Hill. Here, you will eat the button. Most of the day, you will feel normal. Then, when the sun gets low in the sky you will feel different. Do not be afraid when the dark spirits of the night come to you. They cannot harm you. They simply fear the light of day. The dark spirits wish to hide in the night. Their spirit is in the stars. When the stars shine down through the night sky, their spirit walks the Earth looking for the eyes and ears of the one who is looking and listening. They will help you if your road decides they are meant to guide you. After night, the sun will rise in the morning, and you may have a vision. Your vision may be in the spirit of the day. These are the spirits of great wisdom. In the day, the sun shines and gives life to the world we know best. Day spirits ask the most of you, just as the sun provides to the most of life. I will walk home at the setting of the first sun, but you must remain on Sweet Grass Hill until the second sunrise. Your spirit may not come until the second night and you must not desert him on his journey to see you. On the second sunrise, come home to me and I will make you breakfast."

James took the second option. The very next day, James and Paahsaakii walked out to Sweet Grass Hill, and James ate the peyote. His stata was much like Paahsaakii predicted. James felt pretty normal most of the day. Then as the sun was setting, he began to feel different. The little clouds in the evening sky seemed to glow orange and the wind sang the lofty tune of a flute. The sun went down and the glowing clouds walked out of the night sky. It was clear. James could only see the moon and stars and hear the flute. The first night the only spirit that came to him was the voice of God. He said to James

"Build a fire out of wood. The smell of its smoke pleases me."

There were no trees around, but when James looked behind him, a stack of fire wood appeared out of thin air. James built a fire and sat awake the whole night through. Morning came and as the sun burned off the dew, the sound of the flute became fainter and fainter. Then James began to hear the sound of drops of water hitting a pool. He felt fluid in every way. He took shape to his surroundings. In the light of day, the hill, the grass, the clouds all impressed upon him a desired concept of being, and James began to conform to this. James could feel the flow of energy between each discrete object in his environment, and everything seemed to be as one. Energy and spirit seemed to be interchangeable ideas, and the flow of spirit and energy revealed the humble desires of every being in the ecosystem. The sun, the grass, the fire, it all allowed energy to flow however it so chose. James's eyes were open to the attitudes and opinions of every discrete being in the system, and he felt a sense of unity in the common interest of a sustainable, dynamic world. As he browsed the horizon he began to see tiny hearts effervesce out of the grass that covered the plains. They were blue and red and vaporized as they floated up towards the sun. James began to feel himself float up toward the sky with the hearts. He was rising, gaining elevation and aspect, an aspect that could comprehend what fed life and made the people of the world whole. The intangibale things like love, happiness, and ideas, became objects that could be held. He could see the unity between these things, the Earth, the lives that composed communities and populations. Each was composed of spirit, and that spirit, though dynamic, was unified throughout the world. Each leaf, each droplet of water represented life in a colorful variety of forms. He wished everyone could feel the unity he was feeling. He wished everyone could see the desires of nature, and the fluxes of energy. James' Vision Quest was enlightening him with what he sought. His eyes throbbed and his mind melted into a cognition perceiving the architecture of the wind, the sugary smell of the sun, and the wholesome warmth of the Earth. James was content. He thought this would be all the guidance he would need to get through life, but it was almost too ideal, and his Vision Quest was only beginning. James was content. He was glowing with happiness from this heightened state of consciousness, and he was ready to go back home, but remembered what Paahsaakii had said.

    He stayed on Sweet Grass Hill until the sun went down a second time. The peyote was coming in waves. He was feeling very tranquil while the sun was setting. Then as it became dark James began to feel uneasy. The spirit of the day had faded over the horizon, and with it went James's comfort and serenity. He fueled his fire, and as its light danced across his skin, the sight of his lanky arms, knobby knees, and big boney hands made him feel savage. Seeing himself as a brute sparked a primal fear. The comfort he felt earlier was only a mere sense of direction. He was at his starting point, and was facing the finish line, but he was unsure how to negotiate the road between the two points. It was up to James to take the actions required to follow the direction. James began to feel hollow as he heard a coyote howl in the distance. He watched the stars for a second night thinking he would see a visitor approach. The night was cold and the wind blew. The stars seemed to change colors before James's eyes all night. The constellation, Scorpio, seemed to shape-shift and illuminate in technicolor. He could hear the stars twinkling as the light changed from white to blue to green, and back again. It was captivating and was the only thing that seemed to free his mind from the cold wind that blew through him. The wind grasped his ribs, and tried to make him shudder, but James's fascination with Scorpio was so strong that his heart was in sync with the pulsating constellation. Scorpio seemed to drip with color as he roamed the night sky. As James felt his heart beat he could see himself roaming the sky with Scorpio. They journeyed far, leaving James in awe and full of questions. Whatever James asked, Scorpio only replied with "Follow me." They chased the cold from the night sky, and watched down on Earth with a peaceful connection. Scorpio acquainted James with Ursa, Gemini, and Aquarius. When James asked them questions, they only replied "Close your eyes, and watch with your heart." Their adventure together was waning.

James descended from the night sky and bid farewell to Scorpio. As he did he began to get sleepy, but was determined to remain awake. He trotted around his fire, and began to hum gospel tunes he could remember as a child. Then, in the wee hours of the morning, Coyote came to James under the moonlight. Coyote began to talk to James, then transformed into a man with blood-covered hands. James was shaken by Coyote's appearance, but part of him expected such a thing to happen. Paahsaakii told James not to be afraid when the dark spirits of the night come to him. James braved the primal fear, and opened his heart to whatever Coyote was to bring.

"I am the great warrior spirit," Coyote said. "I have come to you because you will one day fight a battle. This battle will rage, but you must not be afraid for you are the only one who can defeat the enemy."

Then as quickly as Coyote came he was gone. James was filled with questions. James felt stronger by his Vision Quest, but the words of Coyote carved deep suspicion into his frame of mind. Likewise, with any man receiving such prophecy, James wanted to know who, what, when, and where he was to fight. Coyote knew where James road would lead, but he also knew that such details as James desired would only cause him to lose focus on what was important. He would lose focus on all he had learned those days on Sweet Grass Hill. As James waited for the sun to rise, the air grew colder then finally the sun peeked over the horizon and James went back to Paahsaakii for breakfast. When he got to Paahsaakii's house, he shared what he saw. Paahsaakii remained stoic and his only reply was,

"What you have seen is yours to own. I cannot tell you when or how your vision will help you, but you may call on it to find the love and strength it showed towards you. You may call on it to find love and strength in yourself. I will say though, it is rare to have a day vision and a night vision. Most people only have one vision. The gods have big plans for you. They hold you close to their heart."

James took what Paahsaakii said with him, and remembered it forever. He remembered it for five whole years as he worked at the butcher shop, but could not fathom what big plans the gods had for James. After spending long days covered in blood with a knife in his hand all he could think was that he was meant to kill someone. Despite his vision and what Coyote, and Paahsaakii told him, he could not stand the idea of plunging his steel deep into someone's heart and ending their life no matter how despicable that person may be. He also knew very little about evil at that time; how evil smelled, tasted, and felt; how it chased the soul, and tormented the mind relentlessly.

For five long years James went to work and came home with the vision fresh in his head, as fresh as the day he had it. He finally had enough of the slaughter house and went home. He was tied up, hands cuffed in blood. He could no longer take 300 pound men coming in to order a whole cow to be slaughtered and butchered. The customer would salivate, and the rancher would see dollar signs. It was all sacrilege to James' integrity. Butchering cows slowly worked against all the unity and vitality of life that were so vivid and so close to James' heart. That unity and vitality was his faith. It was where he drew his strength, but everyday when he clocked in he was actively destroying it, actively working against himself. He left the rangeland of the high plains headed for the mountains and rivers of Appalachia to try to make a fresh start in his life. When he got home all he could find was a ceramic vat and that big red Dodge. Now, hearts floating out of tall grass were not enough to cool his blood. Evil was sinking its teeth into James. He boiled with rage and wondered if anything in his vision truly meant anything at all. All he could think about was that red ooze and how it coagulates and hardens. He would bite his fingernails and taste the bloody crust beneath them. It filled James's mind with visions of greed and gluttony; ranchers driving Cadillacs, and 300 pound men with sweat dripping from the fat that stuck out from under their shirts, scarfing cheeseburgers, and having heart-attacks. The taste of evil drove him to the brink, now he was on his way to the psych-ward in Good Samaritan Hospital.

"Hearts," He thought. "Was I not supposed to find love somewhere? What love was Paahsaakii talking about? This great battle Coyote spoke of. When, where, with who?"

James had nothing but questions in his head and crazy in his eyes. What he did not know is that Coyote was a trickster. Coyote put thoughts in people's heads that drove them crazy and James was no exception. Only time would tell if James's journey would be one in vain.

Chapter 3

When the elevator doors opened, James found himself facing a lobby with locked doors on the far end. The nurse hit the buzzer. The doors, unlocked and James was wheeled into the seventh floor of Good Samaritan Hospital, the mental ward. The place was pure chaos. There were people staggering without direction, people talking to each other, and people talking to themselves. The institutional odor of baby oil struck James's olfactory senses as he gazed at the imprisoning white hallways and dim fluorescent light. The Seventh Floor seemed to creep and lurch with a synthetic texture. James was checked in at the nurses' desk, then was escorted into the psychiatrist's office. The small office had the same synthetic feel as the rest of the Seventh Floor. The bright lights of the office chased James's psyche back into his skull. The pens were neatly aligned on the desk next to a yellow note pad. The stainless steel desk protruded from the walls which were covered by black filing cabinets. James sat patiently for fifteen or twenty minutes then finally a doctor walked in and introduced herself as Dr. Noel. She was a hag of a woman with a hairy mole, a fat ass, and the saggiest tits he had ever seen. When she opened her mouth, the words that came out sounded like they were being strangled out of a duck.

"Now James," she spoke, "I understand you called the cops on yourself. Why is that?"

James hesitated for a minute. Then when he opened his mouth, out came the only thought he had in his mind for the past five years.

"Blood," James replied in the most monotonous voice to ever break a sonic frequency.

"Can you elaborate on that?" Dr. Noel squawked.

"I said, *blood*!" James replied.

"Okay, allergic to any medication?" She squawked again.

At this point James was beginning to get slightly amused. It wasn't the nature of the question Dr. Noel was asking, but more the way in which she asked them. By this point James was envisioning a 240 pound duck with saggy tits on the other side of the desk reading some hokey list that was put together by professionals, you know, people with all the right shit stewing in their skulls.

Dr. Noel continued to ask James questions.

"Have you ever taken any recreational drugs?

"Just blood." James said as he started to feel the edginess of the whole situation wear off.

"Are *you* serious?" Dr. Noel replied. "Is that how you're going to answer *every* question?"

James tried to hold back, but he began bubbling inside and just couldn't contain himself.

25

"I ate peyote once. Fucked me up ten sorts of sideways!" he laughed.

Dr. Noel disgruntily jotted down a few notes then excused James from her office. What James didn't know is that from the moment the paramedics put him in the straight jacket something was growing inside of him. It was his spirit. He finally broke the chains that bound him to the tyranny and oppression of modern society. Launching that ceramic vat through the windshield of the big red Dodge dematerialized the shackles that restrained James from walking his own path. He broke away from the material world by means of its destruction. He finally acted upon an impulse, and even greater, he stood to face the music. It was symbolic. It was a cleansing of the soul. Whatever demons haunted James seemed to vanish after hurling the ceramic vat through the windshield. James was pinned to the ground for too long, and it was about time someone felt the weight of his fist. There was nothing civilized about his role as a butcher, and once he took that first step and hurled that 80 pound ceramic vat through the windshield of the big red Dodge, he began an introspective revolution that allowed his spirit to walk the road it was meant to walk. After the initiation of his detainment, James began to feel a little relieved inside. He loosened up. Life in this place didn't feel so morbid and destitute. That was at a time when James thought he was going to be on the Seventh Floor of Good Samaritan Hospital for two or three days. Tragically, James was greatly mistaken. The doctors saw James as a threat to society. They were bound and determined that he would never have the opportunity to cause further destruction in anyone's life ever again. Despite the very finite extent of his answers to Dr. Noel's questions, he said things that were pretty dark. The mere mention of anything that symbolized violence or hostility was taboo on the Seventh Floor. He lived a life of sifting through death, and that brought him to a place that cloaked his whole outlook on life in a bloody, grotesque vision. He said things that robbed him of the credibility of what the professionals call a "sane individual." His words were ambiguous leaving plenty of room for the professionals to twist them into something more demented than they were. When the little glass house upstairs finally shattered, all the bloody anguish transformed and spewed out of his mind into witty sarcasm. All convention was lost. To James, his great battle had just begun. He decided then and there that Coyote played a dirty trick in his vision. This great battle was not against someone else, and it would not be a bloody one, but it was a battle of a man against society. It had been for the past five years. Whenever James found himself amongst people, he couldn't help but despise what he could see; two hundred dollar sunglasses, and five hundred dollar watches. There they were living the life of luxury while people like James scraped by through life, working the underbelly of society, and had nothing but pain to show for it. He was bound to explode. He sat back and thought about the course of events that had brought him to the Seventh Floor. By the time he was excused from Dr. Noel's office his eyes were as big as the Montana skies. His pupils were so dilated that he looked like he had just eaten a ten-strip of acid. James was swimming in epiphany. When he walked out of Dr. Noel's office, a nurse started looking him over and began moving his way. She was about 5'10" and 120 pounds. When she walked, her slender waist and round bottom popped from left to right, back and forth, as her long brown curls bounced on the white shoulders of her uniform. Her legs screamed up from the floor, and as she leaned in to ask James a question, she pressed her full-bodied breasts against James's quarter.

"Would you like something to eat?" She asked as she fanned her face with the menu. The whole debacle began around 9:30 in the morning and upon reception of the question James looked at the clock and saw it was pushing 6:00 in the evening. Nothing seemed too intriguing about the Seventh Floor aside from this nurse, and James damn sure didn't want to spend all night hungry so he replied with a yes, and the nurse handed him a menu.

"Anything you want, as much as you want!" the nurse explained with her perky little voice.

James looked over the menu

"Hamburger, Steak Sandwich, Roast Beef" he read.

The mere thought of beef made his heart sink as he accepted his reality. This whole damn nation was so headstrong on their damn beef to the gluttonous point of obesity, and James was the one who had to shoulder the grotesque load, slicing meat from the carcass, coming of age with a knife in his hand and blood on his face. He couldn't handle looking at beef on a plate. It would take him to a place he didn't want to go, a place from which he had spent all day trying to free himself. Finally he saw fish on the menu and ordered two fish sandwiches. Someone brought them up about 45 minutes later. James ate them, then he was shown his room, number 135. It had tile floors and smelled of disinfectant. There was much room to get around the shelves and dresser, and a large window laid to the right of the bed with trees overgrown, blocking the view. James was indifferent to his quarters, just happy to lie down. He was by himself, no roommate, and a personal shower. He showered then changed into hospital clothes. The day had worn him out, and as he turned in early and laid down in bed around sundown, he realized it was Friday the 13th.

Chapter 4

Saturday May 14th wasn't much better than the day before. It began with breakfast. The only things James could get down were a banana and a bowl of cream-of-wheat. It felt like mush in his mouth but when it hit his stomach he could feel the raw sustenance. His stomach wasn't turning any more, but he had no desire to eat the sausage that laid on his plate. The past five years developed a man stout with anger towards the world. He was far enough away from Montana that all the blood on his hands and in his brain had been washed away, but it was the greed, the demand for mass murder to provide a fat belly that panged James' temper. The coffee served with breakfast allowed him to loosen up just long enough to take a deep breath, then slowly the room worked him back into a frenzy. He could smell red meat in the air. It made his limbs and body surge with adrenaline. His eyes widened and his scalp tightened. He clenched his spoon with white knuckles as he shivered with excitement. More than anything, it made him feel hollow. The greed of others left him feeling hollow. It left him feeling as though all he had was his vision, something intangible within the material consumer culture. Coyote's words that James would be the great warrior of his people were brewing in his head and in his heart. He was a rebel. He rebelled against the masses, consumption, and gluttony when he shattered the window of the big red Dodge. He *was* a warrior and his enemy was the evil that lives within us all, but this did not make him original no matter how much James might have believed it did. He looked out the window to get his mind off the struggle, and as he did, he noticed the trees and shrubs on the hillside. They seemed be looking in at him. James could see personality and emotion within each plant. Their leaves and branches jutted and sprawled in complementary fashion as if to speak to him. They were not happy that he was locked up on the Seventh Floor. The trees and shrubs were very opinionated in their message. He thought maybe something in his soul spoke to the Earth. Maybe something in his soul had power over the wind and the water and the grass upon the hill. He was pure at heart and his visions were powerful, and ever since his experience on Sweet Grass Hill, he felt a connection with Heaven and Earth that he could not explain. As he looked at the plants outside, and they looked at him, he began to desire power over something in his life. He knew he had power over the herds. He experienced that in the most explicit sense. James was in a dark place. All he could think about was the battle he was to fight. How could he fight this battle against greed from within the Seventh Floor? When he sat and thought about it he felt like he knew nothing. James felt like Coyote had played the greatest trick of all on him. He longed to be back on Sweet Grass Hill with those virgin hands and virgin eyes, listening to the flute and watching the hearts effervesce from the tall grass. Instead he was stuck on the Seventh Floor and waited to be evaluated by the psychiatrist, Dr. Chode.

Dr. Chode was fat, balding, middle-aged white man with thick glasses, and a constant shit-eating grin. His fat belly stuck out of his white lab coat like a pregnant woman's, hanging down over his belt. Sweat was beading on his bald head, and when he opened his mouth, the disgusting stench of garlic, and cigar smoke filled the room, knocking everyone back on their heels. Every time he spoke James could feel him condescending.

It was thick and humiliating. Every word slithered off his tongue and up James's nose, settling in his sinus cavities with a pungent stench that made the hair on the back of James's neck stand up until he was full bore pissed off. In the silence between Dr. Chode's slithering words an animosity grew between professional and patient. His garbled words were thick, and he spoke with a meter that lacked rhythm allowing for many awkward silences. It built anticipation, and removed any degree of comfort that could be found in a well-spoken man's voice. Dr. Chode liked to use the term "lacking control" and accused James as the person of fault for everything that troubled him. Dr. Chode could see the frenzy in James' eyes and found it entertaining. He knew that no matter what James did or said, he was Chode's puppet. Dr. Chode had the final say, and after the way James' reception went, Dr. Chode was going to take James for one hell of a ride.

"So you ate peyote." Dr. Chode began.

"That's what I said." James replied with indifference.

"You know, that makes you dangerous. You obviously aren't in control. You obviously don't know who you are." Dr. Chode pestered.

Dr. Chode looked ready to laugh in James's face, and James was ready to tear Dr. Chode a new asshole. James wasn't the most rational of people. James's entire concept of reality was drawn from experience rather than reason. As extreme as those experiences may have been, they were balanced. Those hours spent covered in blood with a knife in his hand developed a rather savage concept of reality. But, he always looked back on Sweet Grass Hill to bring peace to his soul. About the time James headed home to Appalachia, the tangible was gaining speed upon the intangible, and you could tell that with one look in James' eyes. He was slowly moving in the right direction, edging away from the brink when Dr. Chode began his evaluation. The doctor was pressing, but James remained cool and collected, at least externally, when Dr. Chode said to James that he doesn't know himself. For all James had been through in life, he was perhaps the most self-aware individual Dr. Chode ever evaluated. At the least he knew himself well enough to call it quits in Montana and head home before he drew the blood of another man with his knife.

Dr. Chode was notoriously greedy for power. He liked to stick his dirty finger deep into his patient's mouth and wriggle it until they screamed and cried in such a manner that made all the professionals decide the patient must be committed to a mental hospital. Dr. Chode had countless people committed to mental institutions. After he saw the look in James's eyes and heard his preliminary evaluation, Dr. Chode had a hard-on to stick his finger deep in James's mouth and wriggle it, and show James who was boss. It was a game he liked to play. Long ago Dr. Chode forgot about trying to cure patients and began throwing his weight just to watch the people squirm. He was a good doctor at one point in time, but after a short while he got bored and found his position frustrating, trying to help people who couldn't even understand that they needed help.

After James's first experience with Dr. Chode, James made up his mind. He said to himself that he was going to be as casual and rational as possible. He didn't want to make a long stay on the Seventh Floor, and furthermore he didn't want to be committed to a mental institution. It was

James's deepest aspiration, like many people, to be free. He knew freedom rode the vehicle of knowledge and activity, but James' limited realm of experience left him a little oppressed in the eyes of sane society. He knew a little bit about nature, and a little bit about peyote and Sweet Grass Hill, and a lot about blood and where meat can be cleaved from the bone with the greatest of ease. On the other hand, Dr. Chode had all the freedom that James ever dreamed of. James wasn't about to get emotional over the whole situation and become a slave to people's opinions. Medicine was supposed to be a science based upon facts and solid evidence, but Dr. Chode's opinion of James left James' livelihood hanging in the balance. James was a good dude. He didn't need this shit. He just cut a little too much meat. The peyote didn't help, and Coyote was probably howling with laughter as he watched his trick unfold on James from the heavens. Or was it a trick? Maybe there was a little truth in that mysticism.

James had enough. He knew where he stood, and knew every inch of ground was going to be an introspective struggle with wit and self-control. It was a mind game at this point and James knew he would have to be a bit wilier than Coyote. Spirit got him into this mess, and it was his only hope on getting him out. James needed to appear cool-usual, but what was cool and usual to him was a far stretch to call sane. Blood and peyote conditioned James's mind in a way that any observer perceived James as anxious and wild-eyed. His soul was drowning in blood, and you could see it in his eyes. He was disconnected, and it was time for some assimilation, but he picked the damnedest place to do it. Conformity isn't worth much in the confines of white walls and small tinted windows. A mind could fall deeper into the abyss of psychosis in that environment. The frame of reference to judge your own state of mind was heavily skewed on the Seventh Floor. The only personalities he had to assimilate with were the crazies, or the doctors and staff. Patients complained with each other over their disdain with bingo. The conspiracy theory that the patients were being fed rat poison at night was not uncommon, and many were certain they had worms in their brains. Some of the most sane minds and personalities were those of the plants that he viewed on the other side of the window of the Seventh Floor. It was a limbo but James's situation wasn't hopeless. The staff offered hot beverages every few hours, and there were a few nurses who were sincere and sympathetic. And there were a few patients who hadn't completely lost touch with reality.

James took his time about connecting with the people on the Seventh Floor. The atmosphere of the Seventh Floor was a little intimidating. Even if James had the desire to converse with most of the patients, he didn't have the slightest idea on how to approach them, but regardless he had to make a connection with someone there. He cooled in his room until lunch, then after eating he began scoping out potential allies. The first target was a short, quiet fellow named Ryan. He had on a pair of white slippers that caught James' eye. Ryan looked like a man deep in thought, not perplexed or burdened by the Seventh Floor, but rather contemplative of his own purpose pondering what he had to offer the world and what exactly was he looking for in life. Just the sight of Ryan was calming to James. He was about twelve years older than James, and the most intriguing thing about Ryan was how he distanced himself from most of the people who were totally fruit-loops. Ryan wasn't disfunctionally anti-social. He just suffered from depression, and that made him a bit of an introvert. James approached him.

"How'd you score the slippers?" James asked.

"You mean the shower-shoes? I just asked. They have a shitload in the stockroom," Ryan replied.

"Man, I need something for my feet. Walking around this place in nothing but my socks is killing my knees and ankles!" James went on. "My name's James. I just came in yesterday."

Ryan cracked a bit of a smile and shot back, "That'll happen."

There wasn't a whole lot that could be said between those two. Neither wanted to know why the other was there. It was of no use. Sure it would have been amusing, but when you get down to brass tacks the only substance that was worthwhile in that situation was conversation that held no substance at all.

"How old are you?" James asked

"Thirty-five." Ryan replied, then there was silence. The two men just sat and enjoyed the peace as best as they could. Silence was something James was used to. There was a lot of silence in Montana. It was tranquil, but very lonely, and after a while, the silence left him feeling hollow. Silence let his mind wander leaving him deep in thought, and after some time James found himself constantly pondering companionship almost to the point of obsession. The thought of Coyote that night on Sweet Grass

Hill usually broke that obsessive preponderance. Then his thoughts shifted towards the great riddle.

"How am I the great warrior of my people? What will I fight?"

It took five years and an admittance to the Seventh Floor before James finally began filling in the puzzle. He was to fight the battles as they came. His vision was symbolic and intangible, and he needed to enhance the things in his life that were symbolic and intangible, such as personal relationships. The Seventh Floor was a good place to start but it had its limits. James doubted that he could get where he needed to go from the Seventh Floor, but he figured gentle therapeutic efforts were worth a try. Talking with Ryan seemed to break the ice, but James was a long way from appearing sane.

"One day at a time," James thought. "Nothing I can do now."

Being confined to the Seventh Floor left James feeling a little empty. He couldn't feel the wind in his hair and the sun shine down on his face. He was a prisoner. There was none of that good radioactivity found in organic matter, just white halls and three converging wings of carpeted floors. All the positive energy within the living world was lacking on the Seventh Floor. Patients were removed from the essential relationships that create a healthy mind. James sat in the lounge with Ryan for the next few hours watching CNN. The Midwest was being ravaged by tornados. Watching weather reports was all that made James feel any connection with the outside world, but he was displaced, both physically and mentally. Ryan was watching too.

"Man, God must be pissed!" Ryan remarked. "No sympathy for the Midwest."

The comment struck a nerve with James. Despite all his interest in mysticism and magic, and his experience with Paahssaakii, he never turned his back on his Christian roots and the Christian God, Jehovah. His roots were all that kept him from killing someone after working in that slaughter house for five years. God kept James close and made sure he didn't get bloodthirsty. James was young and receptive, and his environment was well capable of instilling delusions of violence with all the sights and smells it had to offer. Body parts piled up on their way to the incinerator. Dead eyes stared you in the face stealing your breath. The feel of warm blood up to your elbows and the smell of intestines curdled any feelings of comfort you held within. Most of the men James worked with were totally normal, but James was a lonely young man, a transient. He had nothing to bring him happiness. All he had was his limited experience conditioning his whole conception of reality. Every now and then James would look over at Ryan and wonder,

"What would make *him* want to kill? What would make *him* want to destroy something beautiful?"

It was more a question of personal experience than a question of Ryan's rationale and psychology. James had been to dark places, but truly believed that no matter what, good would prevail. No matter what Hells a man may have gone through in his life, he could always lean on truth and righteousness to bring him back from the darkest of places. It was the innate power of the Great Creator that burned bright deep down inside of him and every man. James wasn't as much of a devout believer in Christianity, or any religion for that matter, as he was a philosopher of virtues, and a believer in the human spirit. He believed that humans, as self-aware stewards of this great Earth, we are both entitled to, and responsible for achieving the higher pleasures in life; righteousness, utility, and virtue. By the time James said goodbye to Montana he was beginning to get dangerously close of proving himself wrong and shoving his steel deep into the heart of a human being. Being so close to death for so long was beginning to work away the righteousness, utility, and virtue within James. He felt empty. His day to day did not greet him with evidence of good in the world. Experience was showing him nothing but mortality and mutilation. His beliefs were almost shaded with a crimson hue, but he knew when enough was enough and it was time to come home. James wanted to ask Ryan the filthy questions, particularly what would strike the correct nerve to make Ryan want to destroy something beautiful, but it was of no use bathing in negativity. James thought about the tornadoes on the news and wondered,

"Was it a rain dance gone wrong? Was it the wrath of the Almighty?"

To James's surprise,

"What's your opinion on spirituality and religion?" Ryan asked at that instant.

"I hold faith in the Christian God," James replied "But I have experienced things that make me see the spirit of him in nature, almost to the point of Animism. The sun, wind, water, plants, animals, and soil all have the Holy Spirit. I can see that when I'm in nature." Then James's voice lowered. "But between you and I, that's what this place is dangerously lacking."

James' remark got the wheels turning in Ryan's head. Ryan had never met anyone like James before, but that is not to say that he couldn't comprehend or connect with the comment.

"I can see what you mean" Ryan said. "I used to go out to the lake by myself some nights, and I would sit there and be calmed by the water. And when I would hear the loons off in the darkness I would get this feeling inside of me. I guess it was the feeling of the Holy Spirit like you said."

The two sat deep in thought for a little while, milling over what the other had said. James started to feel a connection with another person. It was simple, and it was exactly what he needed. James soaked in the feeling for a little while. There was a sense of compassion between the two, and more than anything, James just needed to know someone else cared about him. That may have been the toughest thing about those five years spent in Montana: No one cared about his ideas or how he felt. He was just a worker, only looked at for his labors. All of the substance between his soul and that of the people he was around revolved around butchering meat. Eventually the compassion wore off, and both men were too tired to care about talking. James bade Ryan goodnight, and headed off to bed.

James rose at the breakfast call the next day. He ate his French toast and drank his milk then walked slowly to the lounge. He realized something that morning. The days pass slowly. No pleasant excitement, just the dull lapse of time. He realized if he hurried this thing along, he would find nothing but walls. The nurses and doctors were always in a damn big hurry. It got the blood pumping towards no tangible end. James started that day to condition himself towards blocking out all the periphery. Most hours of the day, screams and cries from the patients constantly broke a man's focus. Comfort came in cycles with no sort of rhythm. Just as James settled into his chair or bed, and his mind relaxed, psychotic cries broke the airways creating tension in the mind once again. The doctors would march the halls in packs, and the nurses were constantly buzzing around administering medication and trying to hold conversations with the doctors, patients, and each other. The confines of the Seventh Floor held an energy that grinded away the spirit of those held captive. There was no escape, only scrutiny and antagonism. Nurses forced pills down the throats of the patients. Doctors held evaluations with pointed questions that no patient could give answer with an appearance of temperance and control. At the very least, any person on the Seventh Floor could wear the diagnosis of depression. James was not that lucky, although that was primarily what he was suffering from, depression. The personality of most of the professionals created an interface between them and James that made James appear to be a monster. He was not feeling love so he could not reciprocate the expression. He was cold, and that made him a scary man. He knew that. He knew he could kiss ass and maybe weasel his way out of the Seventh Floor, but he couldn't bring himself to do it. Instead, he would bide his time, and figure what "average" felt like.

After a long, slow walk filled with thoughts, James finally arrived at the empty lounge and took the remote control to the television in his hand. He took the privilege of turning on The Weather Channel. He had the room all to himself. The television was his. At one time he believed watching TV was mind numbing and rotted the soul, but as he sat alone in the lounge that morning, he found an innocent indifference about the practice. He sat and watched the forecast for an hour or so then Ryan walked in. The meteorologists talked about the drought that was beginning to affect the country. James turned his head, and looked out the window. The trees he saw appeared to cry out to him for help. Their leaves weren't wilting yet, but each tree, bush, and plant, knew what was about to come. James wondered would his great battle be one to console the spirit of nature and restore vitality to their lives? James couldn't do anything about it from the Seventh Floor and it panged him so. James was dwelling on the spirit of nature, then images of lakes in the night appeared on the screen and loons hooted through the stereo. It broke James's thought, and struck a nerve in Ryan.

"You know, when I used to go out to the lake at night, and just sit on my tailgate by the water's edge I lost myself out there. You start thinking about everything subsurface, and it's all alien. You can't possibly conceive it but you know it's beautiful. My friends never had me. My girls never had me. But that lake, it had me every time."

It was a comfortable thought, the idea of losing yourself in a moment. Giving the mind time to release and recover from whatever may be ailing it is important. That importance was lost for a long while with

James. Long weeks in the butcher shop never gave him a moment to escape his toil and societal responsibilities. It wore him thin, and the thought of that left anxiety building within James. He felt trapped and needed to do something to get his mind off what was going on in the outside world. A voice called over the intercom inviting patients to the craft room.

"I think I'm going to go color some toads" James said to Ryan, doing his best to force a smile.

James walked out and slowly made his way to the craft room. He hoped that if he diversified his activities, the days would pass more quickly, and he wouldn't feel anxious or trapped. When he reached the craft room he walked into a space with white tile floors, and round desks. The windows were big, bigger than any other room on the Seventh Floor, and James was pleased with this, even a little giddy. There were about ten or twelve patients in the room, and a bookshelf filled with crayons, colored pencils, markers, and books. He saw an instructional book that showed him how to draw a few animals. He picked up the book an took a seat at a desk across from a pretty, young girl. He watched her move the crayons over the page with her delicate fingertips. She tripped the imagination and began to get James all hot and bothered. He shook the sensual thoughts from his brain, and began thumbing through the book of animals. He tried his hand at a bear, then thumbed through the book hoping to find directions on how to draw a coyote. He found none and maybe it was for the best. Besides, the image of Coyote from that night on Sweet Grass Hill was burned into his memory for life. James tried to lose himself in the arts and crafts, coloring and drawing. The prospect of a creative outlet sparked hope.

Though it was bleak hope, it was hope nonetheless. Activity, involvement, it appeared to be and escape. He started coloring and drawing slowly. Then, he'd catch himself holding his breath and scribbling with mania. He'd get the feeling his skin was crawling as his mind raced with thoughts. It wasn't until that moment that James realized how tight his head was wound. Subconsciously, he did get used to the butcher shop, or at least he adapted. His soul and character in the course of that adaptation may not have been maintained at an optimum level. He was working on things in the Seventh Floor. Nevertheless, James would look up at the other people in the room and want to just tear their work to pieces. Five years of working in a butcher shop with no friends or family to come home to will do that to a man. He could still hear the sounds of the meat grinder, and band saw cutting and grinding, filling the room with the smell of fat and muscle. The industrial memories of meat processing held the door open for furious impulses to stroll through James's consciousness. It was trauma that seethed through his brain like oil. The pain itself was manageable to some degree, but ignorance to a person's pain was an even deeper laceration. Ignorance to a person's pain was everywhere on the Seventh Floor. Ignorance on behalf of the professionals was inexcusable, but there was another sort of ignorance on the Seventh Floor, that of the patients. James came to the understanding that it wasn't every patients fault that they were ignorant. Most of the patients didn't have the learning aptitude James possessed, and he soon realized that. He didn't give them the cold shoulder. James tried to be as warm and genuine as he could be, but he was damn sure not to involve himself in a conversation that made him appear psychotic or delusional. He had the sneaking suspicion that eyes and ears were everywhere, and he was damn sure not to let the Seventh Floor get one up on him. Most of the people in the arts and crafts room didn't have a good grip on reality. Some thought they were super-heros. Some had no faith in themselves that they could ever face society or nature and find success. Most of the people on the Seventh Floor were hiding from some aspect of truth, and were delusional because of it. Even the pretty girl James was sitting across from was so deep in depression that everything looked grey and there was a good chance she would never see the beautiful colors in front of her. At least arts and crafts time was a time and place within that prison that was peaceful and therapeutic to everyone. The creative outlet let James's mind wander and forget the walls around him. There was virtue in the symbolic exercise of artistry. It was the process of taking the personal significance of what you see and feel around you and producing something beautiful. The lack of sanity in the art room usually left him yearning for sane conversation with sane people. It left him wondering what Ryan was up to.

It was lunch time. Hamburgers were served and James couldn't bring himself to even lift the beef patty off his plate. He looked around as the whole mental ward gorged itself in the meal while James picked at his peas and pudding. Watching burger grease drip from the mouth of every patient on the Seventh Floor left James feeling a little disheveled like the walls were closing in around him. He longed to feel the sunshine on his face and the wind in his hair. It was only his third day on the Seventh Floor and it was already beginning to break him. The isolation from sensual, Earthly stimulation left him hungry. There were nearly zero sensations that let him know he was alive. He was in some numb, melancholic balance as he spent his waking hours in the prison of the mental ward. He reached out and tried to grasp whatever he could to feel life, but he was having a hard time obtaining those impulses.

After lunch, he walked to the lounge and found Ryan reading a magazine. The Weather Channel was on the television again, and the meteorologists were talking about a drought that threatened the country. The words from the atmospheric scientists got James' wheels turning. He spaced out and began thinking about those effervescing hearts on Sweet Grass Hill. He caught himself before he really began to dwell on the thought. It was a dangerous thought and James knew he couldn't ponder things like that if he hoped to get off the Seventh Floor in any expedient fashion. Dwelling on it too much was sure to take him to a neurotic place, and doing the song and dance for Dr. Chode and the other professionals was a fine line to walk. A single hiccup and he would hear "You don't even know yourself" fall out of Dr. Chode's mouth. James needed to get his mind off of effervescing hearts, and Sweet Grass Hill, and the weather. He interrupted Ryan's reading.

"Do you have a family, Ryan?" James asked.

"Nah, I'm an orphan, and it never seemed to work out with women." Ryan replied

"Don't you desire love? Don't you long for anything?"

"Sure I do, but nothing of this world. How about you"

"I haven't felt love in a long time."

They sat in silence for a while, each thinking about what they had said to the other. Ryan's words hit home with James, and James began contemplating his own desires. He wanted a tangible love, and all of a sudden he felt lonely. He never had a girlfriend. He was deserted by his family, sent out to find God knows what in a slaughter house in Montana. He had no tangible love, only a virtuous road with a righteous destination. Though he had no one to wrap his arms around and lay next to at night, he did have love. He learned things that night on Sweet Grass Hill that filled his heart with respect and kindness, but he was thrown into an economic situation that removed him from where he found belonging and purpose in life. James saw life as the embodiment of spirit. It was a relationship between energy and matter that derived so much beauty. Working in that butcher shop for so long slowly worked at destroying that relationship between energy and matter. Now, the professionals on the Seventh Floor were working further to destroy that relationship. They believed James' concept of reality needed reworked from the ground up. They were robbing him of the most precious part of a human's integrity; their ideas, their beliefs. James held on to his vision quest and all that it taught him, but thinking about the place that was so close to his heart was dangerous in his situation. No one considered it sane thinking, but it was all James had. He wanted to get off the Seventh Floor stat, and go find someone he could share a life with far from all the vices of society. Those nights and days on Sweet Grass Hill taught James the feelings that respect and kindness could derive. It was love that he learned and tasted. Then, he was ripped away from all of that in an instant. He was unsure if anyone loved him in the fashion that he knew was possible, but little did he know, he was as loved as a favorite son. Mother Earth saw something in James during those days he spent on Sweet Grass Hill. She saw an 18 year old virgin man, pure of heart, displaced from his home, and he was out to seek the ethos of a culture that lived, loved, and respected all by the whims of the natural world. Sweet Grass Hill knew what went on those two days and nights five years ago. James had favor deep down in the soul of Mother Earth. She knew he was her great warrior, and his battle was just beginning.

Chapter 5

When James arose to his 4th day on the Seventh Floor, the sight of the white walls panged his heart. The dresser seemed to intimidate and tower over him. He was beginning to get the feeling that this place was bigger and more powerful than he was. James was beginning to get the feeling that this place was going to exact some pain from him. His heart raced and pled for an escape. He turned to the window, but saw nothing but branches. He had to get out of his room, and did so just in time for breakfast. He ate his oatmeal and fresh pears, then made his way down to the lounge. As he passed the nurses' desk along the way, he saw Ryan with bags packed.

"Hey man I'm leaving!" Ryan exclaimed with delight.

It was the happiest James had seen Ryan since he arrived. It gave James hope that he too would be leaving sometime soon.

"That's great news bud. I hope you find what you're looking for out there. Just remember, never let the bastards get you down."

"I think I got it. Virtue, right?"

"Right!"

They shook hands and James continued on to the lounge. James was sad to see Ryan leave, but pleased to see such a beautiful bird uncaged. Ryan was the first man since Paahsaakii that James got to speak to about some of the intangible things that he held close to his integrity. Effervescing hearts and the smells of wood smoke worked their way into James's mind as he listened to Ryan talk. Their words created images, and the images feelings. And as they culminated, James was filled with the notion that he was an individual. He had experienced something special out in Montana. Their conversations restored some of the faith James once had in himself, and furthermore allowed a simple social connection that was crucial for a person's sanity. Interpersonal relationships help define the bounds of truth within our concept of reality. James was lacking these relationships for too long, but Ryan helped rekindle the fire that once burned in James's mind. James wished, just a little, that Ryan hadn't left, but knew it was for the best.

It was sometime after lunch when James heard the rolling voice of a middle-aged man in the hallway. It wasn't oppressive or erratic. It was actually kind of soothing, and the exotic thought of it brought peace and consolation to James's mind after he had told Ryan goodbye. He thought it was another chance at connecting with a sane brain, but he wasn't about to jump to any conclusions before meeting the man. James was slowly bringing himself out of this dither, and Ryan's departure was a direct blow to his progress. He could only hope this new patient wasn't a screw-ball like most others on the Seventh Floor.

The Seventh Floor was a hell of a place to get acquainted with. There were ear-popping screams, and conversations that lacked all logic, but nothing set James on his heels like the people who continuously talked to themselves. The schizophrenics were a creature all their own. The grandeur that the schizophrenics showed was disturbing to watch. Most thought they were kings or gods. They walked, talked, and gestured to entities that only existed in their minds. It was painful and unnerving for everyone to watch, everyone except Dr. Chode. James heard them all hours of the day. They were constantly being inoculated with anti-psychotic medication in hopes of forcing a slumber through all hours of the day. All the professionals, especially Dr. Chode, found great pleasure in twisting stories around the minds of the schizophrenics, and James was careful not to appear in that same frame of mind. John was a man of this condition. He told everyone to "Kneel before the King of Avocado!" And if you crossed John, occasionally he would threaten you with the wrath of his guardian, Shoebox.

James's whole experience on Sweet Grass Hill, and the connection he saw with the bloody hands of Coyote, and the blood on his own hands from the slaughter house had lead him to believe that Coyote's prophecy of a great warrior was true. He believed that tale for five years. Now he was locked up in the mental ward of Good Samaritan Hospital. He wanted to believe Coyote so badly for so long, now James was a mere prisoner being careful not to fall deeper into psychosis. If James wasn't careful, soon enough he might become the King of Avocado, protected by Shoebox.

After Ryan had left and there was a further flux of patients, James was moved to a double room where he had a roommate. The identity of his roommate was a mystery until sometime shortly before supper. James was in his new room just meditating on his bed when the old black fellow he had heard in the hallway earlier walked in with an armful of clothes.

"Sorry sir, I didn't mean to disturb you. My name's Neal."

"No worries Neal. I'm James. I wasn't up to much, just kinda waiting for supper"

"Me too! I can't wait for some grub! Eh, I mean I'm a little hungry myself."

Neal's excitement over their next meal took James for a loop. It didn't put James on edge, but it made him a little suspicious.

"Where are you from, Neal?" James innocently asked

"I'm from around here." Then there was a pause. "I'm from a little bit of everywhere, New Orleans, Chicago, Denver."

"Ever been to Sweet Grass Hill?" James asked.

"Can't say I've ever heard of the place."

"Well, it's in Montana. A man can lose himself for days up there."

Hospital staff wheeled in the supper trays and the patients were called to the dining area. James was a little amused by Neal. Neal made James forget about the game he had to play for Dr. Chode and all the other professionals. Neal's presence was therapeutic to James. When James looked at Neal's face he saw a canvas covered with lines of couth and character. His wrinkled eyelids held eyes that were often blinded by thoughts, locked in a humble stare bound with respect. Neal's eyes weren't aggressive or intimidating, but they were filled with questions. The stature of his lips and jaws suggested that Neal's mouth had the answer to the questions his eyes asked. When Neal walked, he moved with his head down, looking up just enough not to bump into somebody. When you approached him with words, he'd tilt his head and raise eyebrow just a bit before curling his lips and giving a reply. When Neal did answer, his voice rolled with a rhythm that soothed whatever troubles were on your mind. He was exotic, but the two gelled. The delight James saw in his eyes as he sat down in front of his meal revealed truth in the premonitions that Neal was a hobo. Maybe he checked himself in to the Seventh Floor for a few hot meals, a hot shower, and a comfortable place to sleep for a few nights before the hospital caught on to him and released him back into the streets. James sat across from Neal and disinterestedly watched him eat. It pleased James to watch someone enjoy every morsel as Neal did. Before every bite of his steak sandwich, Neal held it up to his nose and smelled it. Then he'd take a rather large bite, and chewed it for the longest time. And, after each bite he'd wipe his mouth, take a deep breath, and smile, then repeat the process. It humbled James and made him feel a little embarrassed as to how far he took what he claimed to be the "trauma" of the slaughter house. Maybe his whole journey had a little more to do with his vision quest and loneliness than it did with cutting meat for 70 hours a week. James decided at that moment he was going to open up to Neal, and he was sure that Neal had some stories to tell. James didn't want to know much, just a little bit. The character in Neal's face, and the feeling in his voice tempted James's palate. He presumed Neal could talk for days about time and space, life and love, greed and hate. He was starved for raw recollection of experience. James thought Neal had plenty of experiences to talk about. That's all that

James was really hungry for; a gripping moment of time and space as seen through the eyes of another man. An experience. When you get down to brass tacks, experience is the best teacher in life. It enlightens us and empowers us with knowledge. James was hungry for just a little of the knowledge Neal had to share, but odds were it wasn't the kind of power James could hold over the head of Dr. Chode, and expedite his delivery from the Seventh Floor.

Chapter 6

When James rose on the fifth day of his stay he was feeling anxious. His mind was at great unrest, and his thoughts were racing. He kept thinking about the slaughter house, and Coyote's prophecy. Being locked up on the Seventh Floor not only left him trapped physically, but mentally as well. He felt hollow and yearned for freedom. The mere thought of his captivity angered James. He felt like a pawn in the game of life, and James began to believe that that was exactly what Dr. Chode saw him as. James wanted to reach out and grab someone by the neck and choke them until their head turned purple, but James knew he had to walk the line for Dr. Chode. It was another dry day outside and James's psyche was beginning to fall apart at the seams. As James peered through the window, out to the hillside, he could see all the plants wilting beneath the hot, dry sun. They were weak and began to wither away. Strangely enough, James saw this as a reflection of his own life. His mind was withering at the hand of the professionals on the Seventh Floor. The longer he went without exposure to the natural world, the worse his condition became. He tried to calm himself by watching TV, but as soon as he sat down, talk of the horrible drought that was striking the nation infected his brain. James began thinking that this terrible drought had something to do with him being locked up on the Seventh Floor. Mother Nature was mad about something, and there was no remorse.

James's purity was a keystone for positive energy to flow across the land, expediting the passage of the Holy Spirit from lifeform to lifeform.

Now his energy was removed from the land he walked, and life was being sucked out of it as a result. The ecology was out of harmony now, and the land was filled with greed and gluttony without a pure heart free to walk to fields. James began dwelling on it. "Maybe that's what all those hearts on Sweet Grass Hill meant?" he thought. Maybe James *was* Mother Nature's favorite son. It was a delusional thought, but Native Americans prayed to the Earth for centuries. The Earth reciprocated that love, and now those believers were few and far between. James caught himself cynically dwelling on consumer culture, and got up and walked out of the lounge. He needed to put some distance between himself and the media. He went into his room and laid down. As he laid there he couldn't get the thousands of thoughts about Montana and his spirit to slow from filling his head. He walked to the end of the south wing and looked out the window. The sun seemed to scorch the horizon, but all James could feel was the chill of the air conditioning of the Seventh Floor. "This is my apocalypse," James thought. Freedom was the only cure for James's ailments. He suffered from psychosis derived from the burdens of First World society. He was asked to provide flesh for thousands, and it got to him. Around every corner, the breath of evil breathed hot on his neck, and it got to him. Now he was locked up on the Seventh Floor and the walls and the professionals were beginning to get to him. The Seventh Floor was its own hell. The place was so confined that time and space lost all correlation. There was so little natural light to give the Seventh Floor proper dimension, and shapes began to shift. Hallways seemed to stretch on into the forever darkness. The ceiling seemed to crush down from above, and the walls closed in from all sides. He closed his eyes, and rubbed his forehead. His thoughts weren't as morbid as they were when he left Montana, but James was definitely not in any better shape. He no longer contemplated shoving his steel deep into the fat hearts that walked the streets of Cut Bank, but he couldn't find the peace of mind that would allow him to live as happily as the masses. There was so much evil thrown in his face that he just couldn't ignore it all. He saw the gentle doe-eyed look in the cattle just before they were slaughter, and he slowly progressed from that look through the hide, and the meat all the way down to raw bone with blood on his face and a knife in his hand. He had no comfort upon his return home. The selfish luxury of that big red Dodge stared him straight in the face and he couldn't ignore its hot breath of evil on his neck. He became the disenfranchised and stood alongside comrades like Paahsaakii, a man deferred by his culture because of his faith in peyote. He stood with comrades like Neal, a man denied of simple pleasures like a hot shower and a comfortable bed because of the value of the almighty dollar. He stood with men like Ryan, who would never find satisfaction in this material world.   James was just a little too sensitive, spiritually, emotionally, and mentally.

When dinner was over, James got a surprise. His mother came to visit.

"I need to get out of here. This place is just making things worse."

"Just give it some time, buddy" she said.

"You don't understand. *I'm getting worse!*"

"James you're scaring me. I don't think you're healthy enough to live at home right now."

James was irritated, and got up and left his mother in the dining hall. He felt abandoned. When he returned to his room, he found Neal sitting on his bed just looking out the window. He looked so peaceful that it brought a reverence over James's soul. James felt energy eminating from Neal that rode a mellow frequency. It undulated with mild amplitude, and a wavelength that connected all five faculties with the heart and soul. James's mind came to ease, and all the emptiness he had been feeling all day melted away when he shared the company of the old, black hobo.

"How can you be so satisfied being in here?" James asked.

"I've had plenty of fast livin'. Sometimes you need some slow. You know, out there isn't always pretty. Livin' on the streets you see a lot of ugly things. Tell me son, what's got you so out of sorts?

"I guess all that ugly in the world got me in this mess." James paused for a second then Neal aksed,

"What do you mean? You're hardly ripe. If you've seen a third of the ugly in this world, then you've been livin' too fast, boy."

"I worked in a slaughter house in Montana for the past five years."

"Tell me, what was so bad about that?" Neal asked.

"I guess being covered in blood, cutting meat for 70 hours a week got to me. I just felt like a mule for all the greedy pigs in this country. I had no one to come home to. I never made love to a woman, and that's no way to spend the last five years of your youth. I just had too much of it all, and when I came home I just felt so angry with everything that I just snapped."

"Greed is the smelliest of all the vices." Neal said. "I've seen men killed over just a few bucks, but you know a man who is slow to anger is more powerful than the mighty."

He took Neal's words to heart. He found an angle that gave him one up over Dr. Chode. The thought of temperance towards everyone and everything that antagonized James was like an epiphany. It sparked hope and confidence in James. Likewise, he felt better just getting what laid at the heart of his anguish off his chest. It was the first time James explained his disposition to anyone in any coherent fashion. Every time someone asked him what the problem was, James was so disheveled that he only gave a round-about answer. Talking to Neal in that moment changed something in James. He quit feeling sorry for himself, and began to feel sympathy towards the people he judged so much. He still wasn't alright. That callousness towards mortality, and Coyote's prophecy still gripped him, just a little less tightly. At least now he was being a bit more straight foward, and it felt good. It was a real break-through along his introspective journey. He felt like he was connecting with reality. He watched the pink sky fade to indigo, then walked to his bed and fell asleep.

Chapter 7

James rose long before breakfast on the 6th day of his stay on the Seventh Floor. He walked to the window of the east wing and watched the sun rise. He stood at the window just watching the orange ball burn through the mist. He stood there for nearly an hour enjoying the peace. It was a comfortable change from the craziness that usually stirred all waking hours of the day. The nurses were doing paperwork, the psychiatrists weren't in yet, and there was a somber vibration humming through the troubled minds of the Seventh Floor. James was optimistic he would be leaving soon. After breakfast he sat in his room waiting for his appointment with Dr. Chode.

"Why don't you talk to me?" Dr. Chode asked.

"I do talk though." James replied coolly.

"No, no."

James was as cool as the deep blue sea, but Dr. Chode was feeling bored and wanted to put the screws to James.

"When are you going to release me. There were people here who only stayed two or three days, then you sent them home. I recovered. I don't feel crazy anymore."

"Ah, so you felt crazy? Look, your parents don't want you. I can't send a crazy man to a residence that doesn't want him."

"If you *keep* me here I *will* be crazy. I don't think you're giving me a fair shake."

That last thought pissed off Dr. Chode

"This meeting's over."

"I'm not done talking to you!" cried James as Dr. Chode walked out of the room. "That bastard! I'll sue him for malpractice when I get out of here!" James thought. He was angry for the rest of the day. He had no appetite and didn't touch a piece of food at lunch. James tried to channel his anger during arts and crafts. He braided a necklace, but the whole while hatred was brooding within him. Everything he touched he wanted to break. Everyone he looked at he wanted to beat the shit out of. Dr. Chode cornered James, and he had James just where he wanted him. Dr. Chode knew just how to manipulate patients he wanted to black-ball; twist words around until the patient becomes so angry and neurotic that no professional would ever believe that they are mentally healthy. James came in a little delusional and detached, now new delusions were forming in his mind, delusions accompanied by an anger rooted in truth. James was in a new slaughter house with a much greedier boss-man. Dr. Chode wanted the butcher to taste the blood and grow eyes filled with bewilderment. Dr. Chode wanted James to stand by as he destroyed something beautiful. His actions sent James further not only into anger but psychosis. James's personal uprising angainst greed was met by a greedy man. Dr. Chode had a thirst for power that could only be quench at the cost of his patients' sanity, and he knew all the tricks. James was in limbo. He was nothing but raw emotion at this point. He needed someone to offer their condolences, but his mother was too naïve to understand what got him into this mess in the first place. All the professionals wanted to put the screws to James, and none of the patients could both understand what was bothering him and sympathize with him at the same time. James began looking beyond Neal for companionship. Everyone who was legitimately insane salivated over the idea of being covered in blood with a knife in hand for 70 hours a week. James didn't dare talk to any of the patients about his peyote experience. It wasn't so much that James understood how dangerous such a topic would be on the Seventh Floor, but he valued it sacredly, and didn't want to pollute the most spiritual experience of his life with a half-baked conversation about peyote. It wasn't about getting high. It was about a realization of the forces beyond humanity. Those forces moved James through the human dimension in such an awkward and uncomfortable manner that any divinity that sided with James owed him something deep. His payment was brewing but it wasn't quite ripe yet.

James was in his room when Neal ambled in as casually as a free man on a Sunday stroll.

"Man, ya got me itchin'. What's this Sweet Grass Hill about?" Neal asked.

"It's a holy place to western Native American tribes, mostly the Blackfoot. You wanna hear a story, Neal?"

"Yeah, sure."

"Long ago before the time of man, when animals could move back forth from the spirit world, all the animals could talk. Then Apistotoke, the creator, created Naapi, the old man. When Apistotoke created Naapi only one animal could keep his power to talk to people. So, to decide which animal could talk, Apistotoke said 'Let there be a great race. Whoever wins can talk to Naapi.' So, all of the animals lined up. Coyote, Tortise, Frog, Sparrow, Buffalo, and many others were all there. Apistotoke waved his arm and all of the animals raced off. Buffalo and Sparrow were far ahead of everyone else. They were closing in on the finish line and Buffalo was in the lead. At the last second, Sparrow flew up and landed on Buffalo's nose, and Sparrow crossed the finish line first. That is why the men and birds can talk together today."

Neal laughed. He liked the story. He was just hip enough to appreciate a good trickster like Sparrow.

"We don't really 'talk' to birds, but I dig that story man. Tell me man, where did you hear that story."

"A medicine man... of sorts. His name was Paahsaakii which means firefly." James replied.

"Cool."

"I've been to the prairie, the mountains, and the coast, but I've never been to the desert. That's one place I'd love to see!" exclaimed James.

"Nothing but sand, isn't it?" Neal questioned.

"Nah, man. I hear in the spring there isn't a place more beautiful, wildflowers, prickly pear, oasis. You just have to watch out for snakes and scorpions at night." James replied.

"Yeah, boy, that sounds nice! Flowers and the warm sun, mm mm mm."

Neal's response cooled James, and got his mind off of things. He was back on the good news. Neal seemed to have that effect on James. He grounded every lofty delusion, reminding James to be humble, and he cooled James' anger with the soothing roll of his voice. Neal didn't know it, but he taught James a fundamental rule of humanity: Never expect much out of people. You won't be angered as easily, and every once in a while a person will greet you with warmth and generosity, and you will be pleasantly surprised. Essentially, Dr. Chode was no different than any other person James had ever met before. He lived to satisfy his own thrills. Energy either forced its way against Dr. Chode or with him. James let the heat of their disputes mellow when it was with Chode, and he rolled with the momentum when it was going against Dr. Chode. Everyday, he walked into James' room and gave him guff and pushed all his button. And everyday James found a way to come back to a cool head. He worked diligently at all the things the professionals said he needed to work on. He was generous with his time and thoughts. He was prudent and patient enough to avoid the traps and treachery laid out before him, but Dr. Chode was relentless. He wanted to see James go someplace dark, some place darker than where he was when he came to the Seventh Floor. Dr. Chode knew post-traumatic stress disorder was a real possibility for James's condition. James wasn't watching people die or killing them, but rather fattening them while he got eyes full of blood for 70 hours a week. An experience like that could leave any man delusional and hostile, but Dr. Chode wanted to see James more psychotic than the schizophrenics on the Seventh Floor. He wanted to see James fall to his knees and wail for salvation with no rhyme or reason. He wanted to hear James have conversations with himself about the most indecent and grotesque things imaginable. He wanted to see James laugh and cry outrageously for no reason at all. He wanted James to feel trapped. By the time James was ready to turn in every night, he beat Dr. Chode at his own game. All James had to do was remember the stories he told Neal. It reminded James of Sweet Grass Hill. It reminded James of the love and power of the Great Judge and Creator. Those thoughts cooled James's head and heart without limits, and James was beginning to frustrate the Dr. Chode. It was a battle of vice and virtue and James was winning.

Chapter 8

The next three days passed with increasing tension. James was getting anxious for his meeting with the professional who would make the ultimate decision whether he was to stay or be released. He passed the time sharing stories with Neal and some of the nurses. All the nurses kept telling James that he made great progress and he would be off the Seventh Floor in no time. When he came in, he was erratic and impulsive. His actions were the result of raw emotion. He fought with his muscles and not his mind. Then, he found adversity in the confines of the Seventh Floor. The isolation was challenging. The social environment was damning at its least. He did some soul searching in the ten days he had been there, and he was in the process of conditioning his mind into something beautiful; an item of temperance and keen rationale. He was faced with antagonism towards the thing a person holds closest to their heart: Their ideas. Dr. Chode worked hard to steal and contort James's ideas, but it wasn't working. James' spirit grew stronger while he was on the Seventh Floor. He definitely was not the same man who came in. He lost all the hatred that had built up from working out in Montana. He didn't hold a man's taste for beef against him. James was beginning to see it as just another sacrifice we make to have pleasant lives.

On the tenth day of his stay it was finally time to meet with the professional. James walked into the cafeteria and took a seat next to his mother. The professional sat opposite them. This professional had no concept of psychological well-being. Her entire evaluation of James was based off of Dr. Chode's records, and she was too blind to see past all of the doctor's bullshit. Her entire understanding of mental health was built around the dogma of western medicine, a dogma written by the "sane" as they observed the "ill." The mind is not something defined by hard facts. It is a product of its environment, something that hungers for harmony more than anything. But, what would bring James harmony? The professionals didn't have the slightest bit of real insight. It was one-sided, and the deck was stacked against James. He had high hopes. He expected to be released and feel the sun shine down on his face for the first time in ten days. He was glowing with unmatched charisma when he walked into the room.

"James," the professional began, "We're meeting here today to discussing how you will be cared for once you are released."

"I don't think I need any further care. Since I arrived ten days ago, I have felt changes in my psyche and a great deal of moderation in my emotions." James rebutted.

"That's good, and that's what we were hoping for but we need long terms results. The Seventh Floor can be a very comforting place. The stress level here is much lower than in the real world. We need to make sure you can adapt and function in society, and maintain healthy personal relationships. Right now your social skills are, well, less than satisfactory according to Dr. Chode"

James was getting the run-around and it was as chafing as sweaty ass-cheeks on long summer's walk. He wanted to call the professional a quack. What she was saying was a lie contorted into the ugliest of beasts, pig-nosed, and yellow-eyed, slithering on its belly, leaving behind a trail of slime. Everything she said couldn't be further from the truth. The stress level wasn't anywhere near comfortable on the Seventh Floor. The small society of all the mentally-ill patients and the greedy disposition of the psychiatrists created vibrations with ultrasonic frequencies so fierce that the strongest of minds would crack under them. It was rowdy and over medicated with psychiatrists hunting and slaughtering patients. It was a treacherous place. At first glance it didn't look like there was much to instigate the emotions, with its big comfortable chairs, air-conditioning, dim light, and white walls. But, once you dig a little deeper it was more chaos than any free man should be asked to handle. It was a circus and Dr. Chode was the ring leader. He had every professional under his thumb, and every patient at wits end. They were diminished to nothing more than creatures of fear and anger.

"When am I going home?" James asked the professional, irritably.

"Well, we thinking you need to stay here until we decide what would be the best care for you."

James got up and threw his chair across the room exclaiming, "This is fucking bullshit! What that lying bastard, Chode, calls care is nothing short of rape!"

James stormed out of the room. The professional suggested to James's mother that he be committed to a mental hospital, and she begged and pleaded the difference. It wasn't a good day. James finally cracked and had no way of venting his emotions. He couldn't bear the thought of staying on the Seventh Floor for another second. He heard the sirens going off in his head, just like the day the authorities brought him in. James was filled with adrenaline, and only saw two options: kill Dr. Chode with his bare hands, or escape from the Seventh Floor. James waited near the lobby, then, when the door opened from the outside, he rushed through and caught the elevator before the doors closed. The nurses on the Seventh Floor notified security, and James knew they would be waiting on the ground floor for him, so he hit the stairs at the fifth floor and headed down. He made down two flights of stairs, then, as he was rounding the corner he was met with 50,000 volts from the security guard's taser. He fell to the ground and didn't have anything in him to overcome the shock. It hurt, and it hurt bad, but James believed with every fiber of his being that it was the best decision he had made in five years. It didn't work, but the plan deserved an attempt, and James put forth the best effort he could. They strapped him to a wheelchair and took him back to the Seventh Floor. The nurses gave him a heavy injection of anti-anxiety medication. In his room, he was guarded by security until lunch time.

James was served lunch and as he sat before his food he couldn't have been more disinterested. Out of shear spite and the longing for the comfort of Sweet Grass Hill and the Paahsaakii, James decided then and there that he wasn't going to eat a morsel of food until he was released. His fasting began.

Chapter 9

(second day of fasting)

On his 11th day on the Seventh Floor, James awoke to hunger pains. As he sat up in bed and slowly gained consciousness, he thought about the butcher shop, and the big red Dodge, and the Seventh Floor with Dr. Chode and all the other professionals, and all the hunger in his belly melted into a stew of pure rage. James clenched his pillow between his teeth and tore at it like a dog until he was exasperated. He sat in bed and listened to his beating heart. Slower, slower, slower, slowly he could hear the muscle thump in chest, and he thought about the blood coursing through his veins. The thought of blood reminded him of Montana, and the slaughter house. Images of the crimson liquid spewing from the throats of cattle raced through his mind, and those thoughts made James appreciate life and feel whole for he was alive. He slowly accepted reality for what it is; complete imperfection. James began to accept that there never was, nor ever will be a tangible utopia. The means to every end involves sacrifice. Someone or something has to lose in the process of every gain. Wade understood that and accepted it, and wanted James to understand this as well, but the sacrifices that James made for the past five years were raw, too raw. James just wished that everyone who wanted to put meat on the table would have to see their dinner go from beginning to end; from living creature to entre`. He wished that everyone knew the smell of blood, and the sensation you feel through your hands as you remove the skin and slice the meat. He just wished there was a balance among those who made the sacrifices and those who enjoyed the luxuries. If there was balance, maybe the world would revolve a bit more harmoniously. James wanted more than anything to just feel as though everything was in place, just as it should be. The power was not in the hands of the wise, and James was going to make every effort to change that. He spotted the flaw. The human-race will always succumb to vice, and the innocent will always be the primary victims. Once again there was no balance and no harmony. The fruit of temptation was driving desires of lust and gluttony. The strong fed on the weak, but how strength was measured all depended upon whose lenses you were looking through. A man who separates himself from his needs and desires of the mortal realm transcends the grasp of his captors. He who needs nothing is free from everything. James began to see this but his emotions were not yet completely at peace. He had not yet escaped all that truly restrained his soul. He was separating himself from those things, things like food, love, money, and freedom. Money had not been an object to him in a long time. He was learning to ignore the biological demands of food. Love and freedom were objects of the mind. James was not truly trying to give these two things up. Furthermore, to forfeit these two would only weaken the soul, but how James would define freedom and love was about to change. The way James defined love and freedom would determine if his soul would be at peace. The professionals were trying to put *their* definition of love and freedom in James' mind. They did not agree with his definition. They were inflicting savage wounds to the intangible aspects of James' being. *Who were these professionals to throw James under the bus for pure entertainment?* He didn't deserve this. There was a blood thirsty monster lurking on the Seventh Floor, and that was the only thing James was sure of. He thought he had beat Dr. Chode at his own game, but James began to feel defeated. He thought he showed enough couth and self control to persuade the rest of the professionals on the Seventh Floor that he was sane, stable, and happy. That wasn't the case, and the thought of his detainment seemed to be overwhelming. What game did he have to play? How could he win? Nothing was making sense. All he could see was the lust for power this old, fat, bald guy had. Dr. Chode wanted to mutilate James' mind, feast on an innocent victim. James felt helpless. The professionals wanted to rip away what James held so dear to his heart. Nothing made sense on the Seventh Floor, and that made it impossible to feel the least bit of comfort. He could feel the walls of the room closing in around him. He felt nothing, but hunger pains, and those sensations fueled feelings of anger. His emotions were a thorn bush, red with hate, and a grizzly texture that curled, and knotted, tearing flesh from limb, sprawling across the expanse of the horizon. It crept up, constricting his throat making his heart race, and his lungs short of breath. His eyes got big and his hands became heavy. He could feel the adrenaline. He was ready for a fight, but the ring in which he was to do battle in was not one that welcomed fury. His arena was a place of patience and wisdom. Could James achieve the fitness that such a victory required? Could he find peace in Hell?

The call came over the intercom that breakfast was served. James had no intention on eating, but was feeling restless nonetheless. So, he walked down to the lounge and turned on the television. The television seemed so vivid in the fluorescent light, and white walls, but was clearly unnatural. It was light of an alien wavelength to James. The voices that came out of the stereo seemed squelched from their microphones. It numbed the brain and dulled the senses. Nothing seemed stimulating except for the message that was being delivered. Once again the news kept talking about how all of the country's crops were dying from drought. The vegetation pled from the hillside, crying out to James to bring the rain. Their faces of branches and leaves begged with withdrawn, withered faces, begging in despair. James thought to himself,

"We'll never get it right. Reality? That's just a thought that's gone to waste."

Ryan's words started to ring clear in James's mind. God *was* mad with society. With everything that was going on around him, James couldn't help but feel the end was near, and he couldn't care less. The feelings and care delivered to him were reciprocated back towards the entire world. Love feeds love, but the white walls, fluorescent lighting, and the seven stories between him and the Earth had its way of obstructing the vital spiritual energy that he so desired. All he had were memories of his vision. He started thinking about what Coyote said to him.

"A warrior? Fight for what?" James thought. "My own mother doesn't even love me enough to fight the 'professionals' up here." Little did he know, James was loved, but by none more than Mother Earth and Father Sky. James was sick of thinking, but unfortunately his thoughts were all he was left with. It all stewed in his brain into a soup that lacked body and sustenance. His thoughts were as malnourished as the cold dry desert, and brewed nothing but useless emotions. He stood up and walked out of the lounge about an hour after everyone was done eating breakfast. As he walked out of the lounge, James saw Neal with bags in his hands.

"What gives?" James asked.

"Doc said nothing's wrong with me, and, uh, I have to leave."

James knew sooner or later the professionals would see through Neal's lie, and find out he was just a hobo looking for a hot meal and a bed, but James had hoped he would have been sent home by the time Neal was kicked out. What was going on around James denied every law of social dynamics he had ever come to understand, except for one; the strong will always feed on the weak. Everytime James came close to appearing just as he needed to be to prove to all the professionals that he was sane and competent, the professionals sunk their teeth in deep delivering phenomenal wounds. It seemed as though no good deed went unpunished. Everyone was out to get theirs. The patients tried to prove just how crazy they were, and tried to instill fear in the professionals by doing so. They would spit and bite as the professionals, intimidated, put their dirty finger deep down inside the mouth of every patient. James was not exempt from this bit of science. From the time he stepped foot on the Seventh Floor he instilled fear upon every professional that caught word of his name. He was guarded, but more intelligent than anyone he shared words with. He had more experience in the foulness of reality than most men he came across. A butcher will have that. The slaughter house haunted him. Its memories gushed and throbbed in time with negative energy. James's occupation was to practice what stimulates that disgusting feeling that makes you gag deep down inside. He did it all, execution, gutting, skinning, quartering, butchering, and disposing of scrap. Everyday for five years it was the same thing: look an animal in the eye then murder them and prepare them for the table. The activity spawned a parasite that ate away every last bit of comfort in his life. At first it was just while he was at work, then after taking so much of it, he began carrying those feelings home with him after he clocked out. Before, James's was a man appreciative of art, life, and beauty. But, after spending those five years butchering, and slaughtering cows, life lost its luster. He felt the pain of the victim, and it ate at his heart until his state of mind was a constant, frenzied mania. He was the underbelly of society, and now the professionals of the Seventh Floor were face to face with James day in and day out. He was now the meat on the chopping block. The professionals wanted to see how far they could take it and how long they could handle it before they could no longer look at the man straight in the eye and had to send him off to another institution just say that they served him justice.

By the end of his 11th day on the Seventh Floor hypoglycemia had begun to set in. The hunger melted away. Everything around him looked different. Things were vivid, even in their dull light. When he laid down in bed that night, the bed felt different. He seemed to float above it. James believed that if he could detach himself from the matrix that imprisoned him, fiber by fiber, he would no longer feel the oppression of the Seventh Floor. The laws of the Seventh Floor were limited in their domain. They were created by men, and a man can only control so much. They could not control the fire that burned deep down inside the soul of a patient. James's soul was lit and this fire was beginning to transcend.

That night James drifted off into a vivid wonderland of dreams. He was high upon an alpine meadow, and as he watched the adjacent horizon of forest, the trees and grassland came alive, dancing to the rhythm of the day. All the vegetation glowed with electric, neon light, beckoning James to come, play, and be alive with the Earth. He crossed the valley and began walking through the forest. As he did, he saw faces of the most profound spirits that ever communicated with humans. Buddha, Jesus, Vishnu, and Apistotoke all came to James and told him he was to be the great warrior of his people, just like Coyote told him that hallowed night on Sweet Grass Hill. He held conversations with the weeping trees and bushes he saw on the hillside from the Seventh Floor. None of the spirits gave James definitive answers, but when he asked them questions, they suggested he look in himself and he will be sure to find what he is searching for.

Chapter 10

(third day of fasting)

When the mind finds itself amidst a deep sleep it ventures far off beyond all reason and laws of nature. The exterior-senses shutdown, and the consciousness parades in bizarre directions across an infinite extent. During the first night of James' fast he began to transcend in his sleep as he could feel his consciousness leave his body and travel all over the world. He could see evil brewing in all corners of the globe. Oppressed individuals, and oppressed families, and oppressed societies all came to the fore front. The hands of greed wrapped their fingers around the weak and disenfranchised, and squeezed until all vitality was wrung out. It was all a power struggle between the righteous and the wicked. It was James' struggle. And, although it was his struggle, he was not alone in feeling the crushing hand of greed coming down on him. Tyranny was an expression of some ideal image tyrants tried to embrace by mentally and emotionally distancing themselves from the innocent ones. The affliction of pain was tantalizing to their evil minds, bodies, and spirits. It was like an infection that once began would continue to grow and fester into something abominable. Free thinking was seen as dangerous to the tyrants. They saw it as tool of love, peace, and equality. It was a tool the meek could use to perpetuate the good in the world, dangerous things to a tyrant. James found greed the most disgusting of all vice and Jesus Christ found compassion towards James through this. Christ believed that James could be the great peacemaker of his people. James' rage left him so disheveled that he would be righteous in the face of any enemy. He had the vivid insight to the chinks in the armor, and exploited them. He felt exacting pain for so long that understood exactly how to deliver such pain. He knew how to take the shots that hurt the most. Belittling any man was no challenge. All that stood in the way was punishment, but he was so disgusted that he lost all fear of punishment. His psyche was a rock painted in a calm, blue hue. It was harmless at first glance, passive, but once hurled through the air, it was sure to strike down the wicked with great malice. James was so detached by this point that all the professionals considered him psychotic. He was a danger to their greedy ways, and though the professionals did not detect this on a spiritual level, they all felt nervous when they came face to face with James. He used words like 'you', and 'your desires' with exacting sharpness. Christ spoke to James that third night of his fast.

"The Lord favors he who is prepared."

James woke that morning feeling a little anxious. It wasn't the walls closing in on him. He had come to grips with that. It was all that spiritual contact in his dreams that set him aloof at the dawn of his twelfth day on the Seventh Floor. The blue rock was stirring. Breakfast was served and James refused to eat in preparation to whatever evils he was to face that day.

Dr. Chode came to James's room early on the twelfth day. He started with speed, and jumped on James hard, right from the get-go.

"You threw a chair at a counselor, tried to escape, and now the nurses say you're not eating. You need to have *respect,* respect for the people around you, and respect for yourself."

James could hardly stomach this hypocrite.

"What did you have for supper last night?" James coolly asked.

"That's none of your business," Dr. Chode Replied defensively. James asked again.

"What did you have for supper last night?" James asked with conviction this time. Dr. Chode knew he was not going to get anywhere unless he answered the question.

"I had prime rib," Dr. Chode replied.

"Do you fully understand the sacrifice for that meal? Have you ever smelled a butcher shop? Do you know what dried blood feels like on your face? I know respect. Respect is sacrifice for the good of the community. It's kind of the antecedent of greed. Do you know what greed is?" James had Dr. Chode backed into a corner and on his heels at this point. "Respect is a utility of morals. Respect is being a peacemaker, not just taking what you feel entitled to and raping everyone in your path, but you wouldn't know about that. You're too busy and content with sticking your dirty finger deep down inside the mouths' of those you're supposed to be helping."

Dr. Chode was red in the face.

"Keep it up and I'll send you to the funny-farm! This meeting is over!"

Dr. Chode walked out of the room embarrassed. James won the battle, but was far from winning the war. James knew well and good that if he kept attacking Dr. Chode every time they had a conference, things would not end well for him, but he couldn't help himself. Every time he saw that greedy bastard, James blacked out and his mouth would just move spilling words out that he had no control over. It wasn't like him. James was always a soft-spoken young man, but he began to lose his timid disposition on the Seventh Floor. He was backed into a corner and the primal instincts were taking over. Despite his vulgar display of testicular fortitude, James wasn't getting any closer to being released. If anything, he was digging a deeper grave, but James was beginning to care less and less every day about how soon he was to be released. His debacle was beginning to strike nerves deep down inside of himself, the same nerves that that big red Dodge, and that butcher shop in Montana had struck. James once again found himself in the belly of all that was wrong with the world. So much power was put in such few hands that it had an astonishing ability to strike down the livelihood of the meek and mild masses. James was so detached and disheveled at this point that vengeance was all that was on his mind. The thought of beating the shit out of Dr. Chode had crossed his mind, but that was too easy and too simple. It would only allocate more oppression onto the innocent and righteous. No, Chode was a smart man and there are better ways of inflicting pain upon intellectuals. James would get Chode into a corner every day that he performed his 'check-ups' on James.

Meanwhile, there was much sitting and waiting to be done, and evil rides on idle time. James caught himself holding pantomime conversations with the trees and shrubs he could see on the hillside. His whole stay on the Seventh Floor, James watched as they cried out to him, and every day he could see the expression in their leaves and branches become more and more desperate. The least he could do was acknowledge their pleas and cries. He'd make faces and mouth words, but about the time he began making hand gestures he caught himself at the thought that someone maybe, and probably was, watching. James may have been Mother-Nature's favorite son, but it was a far cry to call him safe from the wicked.

The Seventh Floor had a way with warping minds into a muddled tapestry of misdirection, and James was no exception. All that fluorescent lighting probing down the vanishing corridors coupled with the constant smell of baby oil clenched the mind with a wretchedness that screwed so tight that not a single iota of rationale remained. James was a natural man trapped in a synthetic prison. The aromatics oozed through the air, sterilizing the thoughts that filled the warranted minds of the Seventh Floor. That damn scent started to work on James. It didn't stimulate raw disgust like the mild radioactivity of all the blood in the butcher shop, but the perfume of baby oil echoed in every dim nook and cranny of the Seventh Floor as if to say 'We will harbor you away from every stitch of mature thought and thinking that you have ever developed. You WILL NOT think for yourself'. James tried to walk a straight line as his senses began to lie to him. He stumbled across and began to loath the floor he was walking on.

Each night James's dreams became more vivid. Each night James felt closer to the one true God and every divine spirit in this dimension and beyond. When he came to in the mornings, he felt pure with a mental clarity approaching the realm of nirvana. This clarity was not without sacrifice. It wasn't so much the hunger in his belly that pained him but the sense that someone out there was out to get him. James felt the prowess of evil breathing hot and heavy down his neck. He was not afraid, but he was beginning to get excited. After five years of being covered in blood for 70 hours a week, he became accustom to the wicked and the restlessness that wickedness elicits. On the fourth morning of his fast James sat up in bed and saw a vision. Naato'si, Sun God, was peering down on him with skeptical eyes. A brilliant iridescent glow filled in through the windows and through the walls. The sight of such light sent the eardrums singing. Naato'si's face couldn't be perceived in completeness. As James embraced the light and exploded with life inside of his skin, he was limited by his perception. What James *could* gather was a sense of encouragement, a sense that should he battle evil, he would not be alone. Then as abruptly as the vision of Naato'si hit James' consciousness, it vanished. James rubbed his eyes then got out of bed. He felt a somber peace about him, but as soon as his feet hit the ground, pain surged through his joints. His knuckles felt like they were slammed in a door. His knees and shoulders exploded with arthritic pain and his neck stiffened like a rod. Hypoglycemia crossed his mind, but James thought to himself, "I would rather die than eat one more morsel of food in this hell." James took a couple of deep breaths and moved about, slowly shaking his wretch. He walked over to his window and watched the sun slowly change from orange to bright yellow as it rose in the morning sky. James wondered if Naato'si was still watching him as he shone brighter and brighter. Then James began to think of Jehovah, his Christian God, the god he was supposed to put before all others. James was faithful, but the prospect of the Tribal gods was intriguing, and he couldn't help but wish for their sympathy and power and guidance. His mind was a mélange of mysticism. James became something of a crossroads for the divine. He could feel supernatural powers surge within him, but they weren't all positive. And, the accumulation of his oppression ignited the possibility of voodoo and black magic within his mind. James felt pain and heard the eeriest whispers in his sleep. He didn't know what more to make of it than evil, but as he milled the idea over in his mind he couldn't think who he had crossed that would play black magic on him. He offended the professionals on the Seventh Floor, but they were all too spiritually detached to give any energy into voodoo. Things were getting weird, but it was exactly what James asked for, five years in the making, ever since he ate that button of peyote on Sweet Grass Hill, whether he knew it or not.

    The pangs of the spirit world were beginning to encroach on James. His soul was purer now than ever before and evil never passes an opportunity to corrupt the innocent. When James decided to detach himself from his mortal needs and mortal desires, he became a vessel of spiritual energy beyond what the Vision Quest had bestowed upon him. All day James felt extreme pain throughout his body and as he walked the halls of the Seventh Floor. The real challenge was just beginning. He knew he would hallucinate if he kept fasting, but he was bound and determined to keep it together. He craved the clarity he was feeling. The boundaries of good and evil seemed so distinct, and there seemed to be no grey area. Every stitch of reality was either a product of vice or virtue. Dr. Chode, the professionals, the big red Dodge, and the slaughter house embodied vice. That he could always see, but for so long positive energy had been just beyond his line of sight. James was beginning to find virtue and righteousness in most things in his immediate environment. People were what mattered. He was beginning to see that. They were simply a medium of consciousness and energy. The medium through which vice and virtue traveled was inexplicably innocent. It was the intangibles that carried weight. The consciousness carried weight. The intangible id of the mind exposed the quality of energy passing through a person. So many of the patients on the Seventh Floor cried out in pain from the negative energy inflicted upon them, mostly from Chode's greed. Greed was evil because it put the majority of strength in the hands of a few and was less evenly distributed among the populous. It brewed in darkness and spewed out as wrath. Wrath seemed to be an unwarranted display of strength of the powerful over the weak. They were left helpless, caged in their prison, and denied a fair shake. Pride robbed the commonwealth of due respect. People might argue that money is the root of all evil but James saw through that bullshit. Money had no consciousness. It was just a medium of power, power an individual might be able to hold over others, but showed a complete lack of power over one's self. Virtue burned bright in James's eyes. He seemed to glow in the presence of honesty and charity, and other such admirable ambitions, but he found himself in the cesspool with no way out. His methods of striking down the wicked would be hard fought and would be with great sacrifice. Fasting was no direct action against all the professionals that oppressed James, but it was a means of reaching a place that no one could remove him from, a place that was marked by the holy and the pious.

Chapter 11

(end of the fourth day of fasting)

As one day wormed its way into the next and James' fast continued, his concept of time dematerialized. He had experiences that lasted only seconds, but seemed to last for years. Stream of consciousness passed through his mind with eternal length and eternal depth. James was breaking through to something substantial in the mind and in the spirit. The newness of his thoughts were hard to conceptualize and understand. Space was beginning to appear unnatural, and its relativity to time was losing context. James recollected the visions and dreams of negative energy from his sleep. He dreamt of tall, dark silhouettes smiling with mouthfuls of diamonds as they beat bodies kneeling before them. He dreamt of motherless children drowning in their tears. He dreamt of the faces of animals, wild with fear and bewilderment. He dreamt of dying forests, and dusty plains. They were all filled with the hiss of evil, and cries of the innocent. They smelled putrid, like rotting flesh, and flickered with sparse, dim light. When he thought about them during his waking hours, faces and figures spoke and danced about in his mind. He could hear his heart beat once, then scrolls of dialogue were spoken before he could hear his heart beat once more. The thought of such things left him wide-eyed as his consciousness struggled for comfort. He sat paralyzed reeling in words of the evil that spoke to him, as he gasped for breath, slowly feeling the sweat ooze out of his pores, just waiting for the fear to break. He had experiences so gripping that whatever spirits and energy worked their way into his being created sensations so profound that an instant seized him and nearly froze him in his consciousness. James's eyes had been opened to just a bit of tyranny in the slaughter house, but fasting on the Seventh Floor was beginning to reveal the ugly truth to him in whole. There was so much evil in the world that we never see. James was no exception, but as he left the bounds of mortality, he began to envision wickedness in full. Nothing could have prepared him for the fear and pain that such visions would bring to the young man. He experienced them with sympathy. He became vexed and emotionally drained, but he never panicked. He simply focused on his own situation. He only moved towards fixing the things that were under his control. Wickedness tried to instill fear into James, but he just let the energy pass through him, stone-faced.

The energy would come in waves, positive, negative, then positive again. While James was at peace, the whole day would pass in what seemed like seconds to James. He would sit next to the windows at the end of one of the halls on the Seventh Floor, inhale at dawn, and exhale at dusk. The positive energy within James brought him inner peace. It was warm and comforting. It was an energy that encouraged him and gave him faith in what he was trying to accomplish. He was learning how to multiply his energy, turning small into large. He did not want anything dwelling on discomfort. He would simply wait until he felt the ebb of positive energy, and flow with it, allowing the momentum to build as he carried on. He felt harmony with the world that laid beyond the walls of the Seventh Floor. There was a feeling of naturalness that James developed those nights on Sweet Grass Hill. It was an understanding of spirit and energy that was constant throughout the universe. It was an assertive position in space and time that conserved and sustained the spirit of all that is right and good. He could look out the window and feel the rhythm of the day. Every biological and psychological function within James ebbed and flowed with each wavelength of light, sound, and warmth of the day. Each breath, each second seemed to drift by unnoticed until the cycle of time made full circle. Time ran in cycles. Each moment was significant to what was to come. It created a palimpsest. Each moment built on the last. Space deformed, but time began to make an impression on James as he dove deeper into the spirit world. His perception of velocity was quite askew as he left his Earthly desires behind. He desired nothing, but gained insurmountable connections with what is right and just in the world. Dr. Chode didn't see it that way.

In Dr. Chode's eyes, James was getting more and more psychotic everyday. To James advantage, he couldn't be shipped off to the funny farm until he had stayed on the Seventh Floor for at least thirty days. It was now a staring contest. James could feel the energy from Dr. Chode ebbing and flowing with an ultrasonic frequency. The mere presence of Dr. Chode was irritating to James at it's most comfortable. He never let James simply be. He was always analyzing James, and James just wanted to sit and cogitate. Dr. Chode knew James was fasting and knew some of the side-effects of hypoglycemia, but Dr. Chode never had a patient hold out for more than two days. He expected schizophrenic behavior from James, but got none. Dr. Chode was smiling inside when the nurses would report that James had not eaten, but James remained so cool and collected that Dr. Chode could not pin a false diagnosis on him.

Dr. Chode was getting impatient with his favorite victim and could do nothing to make his life anymore of a hell. Dr. Chode would roam the halls everyday looking for James to be acting psychotically, but only found him sitting in the lounge or in his room with eyes closed and a peaceful smile on his face. James's dreams were so vivid and gripping that he spent most hours of the day meditating, connecting with the spirit world. When he went to sleep at night, he could disconnect himself with bounds of this realm, and find spiritual energy in every object in the universe. Every object in creation held an energy and consciousness that was unique and significant. Sun, soil, rain drops, and blades of grass spoke their souls to James. He was in a frame of mind that could listen to, and understand their voices. Energy was personified. It had a face and a name. James found spirit in the energy of subatomic particles and that spirit was transformed as those particles joined with and separated from each other. Matter and energy were all a product of spirit. Every object held a unique aspect and direction. Each object had a consciousness. The universe had a consciousness. Energy and consciousness were infinite. James could be as small as that button of peyote or as large as the night sky. He ran among the stars, and hid between the blades of grass. Fasting opened a world of infinite possibilities to James. He gave up on trying to socially connect with the other patients of the Seventh Floor. Most of them were so far out in left field that no concept of a functional citizen made any sense to them. Purpose, to most of these people, was not to be a part of the world, but rather to be apart from it. They reeled in mania until it produced anxiety so thick that every reaction was erratic, and produced nothing but disorder. These people were the meek, the weak, the conspiracy theorists, and the fugitives. James made no ground with any of them. It wasn't for lack of effort, but James came to find that rationale was something of a blessing. James may have been a little overboard with his condescending disposition of society, but he did understand that everyone was only human. This leveed no compassion to the wicked , but he did learn to forgive as he matured. As time went on, James found himself sympathizing with the patients of the Seventh Floor, but his disgust with all the professionals seemed to keep adding up. On the Seventh Floor, James was starved from the physical manifestation of everything he believed in. All the virtues that he built his belief system around were intangible from his vantage point. He was restricted in the cage of the Seventh Floor, kept from touching the embodiment of the spirit that so moved him. He could not feel the velvety petals of the flowers, or the warmth of the sun. Without the body, spirit could only be held fast in the mind and soul with blind faith. It was easy to connect with the spirit world out on Sweet Grass Hill, but it was a little tougher on the Seventh Floor. All James had on the Seventh Floor were people with cracked up ideas. Strenuous attempts had to be made by James to connect with what brought him peace while he was on the Seventh Floor. He looked out the window at the trees and bushes as they cried to him. James could do nothing for them. The most he could do from the Seventh Floor was find spirits in his dreams that brought harmony to nature. There was no harmony on the Seventh Floor. At first the professionals were making a lot of headway keeping James from connecting with what brought peace to his soul, but as time went on James found the cracks in the wall the professionals tried to put up. He prayed. He meditated. He fasted. He dreamed. James was beginning to find nirvana in his own hell, but it was all an intangible, symbolic metaphors for all the virtue that brought structure to his psyche, that is until Ron A. was admitted into the Seventh Floor sometime during the thirteenth night of James's stay.

Chapter 12

(fourth day of fasting)

On the morning of his fourteenth day on the Seventh Floor, James rose from bed and did his usual ritual of meditating after watching the sunrise, then he did something different. When the call for breakfast came over the intercom, James moseyed down to the cafeteria and took a seat across from a new face, Ron A. Ron A. had crew-cut hair and tattoos all over his arms, but something about his appearance spoke to James. James could see Ron was a man well-seasoned with the likes of war, and even though James considered war nothing more than a vile struggle of power between nations, he had something of an admiration for Ron. Ron and James were both served their food, but James once again didn't touch a morsel. Ron inquisitively asked James,

"Why aren't you eating?"

"I'm fasting." James replied. The expression on his face told Ron his mind was elsewhere. It was a calm look of focus. James was centered. That was all the information Ron needed. The military conditions the mind to only desire the information that you are told, and be satisfied with that. In that realm of that reality, more information than needed can only breed trouble for those in the know.

Something in James struck Ron's interest. Ron was a man who spent considerable time close to death, and maybe he could smell the blood encrusted under James fingernails, but something in James brought crude comfort to Ron just sitting across from the boy. Maybe it was something intangible. Maybe it was the shared belief between the two that good will always prevail. Ron was suffering from night-terrors. That's what brought him to the Seventh Floor. Everynight he woke around 3 AM and felt as though the Devil was breathing fire down his neck. Like James, Ron was brought to the Seventh Floor against his will because he was beginning to scare his family, and fulfilled their wishes to seek treatment. Ron was familiar with the filth of such a place as the Seventh Floor from being treated for post-traumatic stress disorder, and he wanted to keep a low profile, but a man always needs a friend, and in this case Ron decided then and there that James would be his friend for as long as he needed him.

In war you see things that no man should be asked to handle. James didn't see those things to the degree Ron had, but nevertheless James spent many an hour engulfed in a rather grotesque end of the spectrum. Ron and James seemed to connect on a strange and unusual wavelength. The energy between the two was saturated in a cold hue. It was such low-frequency that it was bothersome to anyone else. Its discomfort was akin to being stared at, but James and Ron somehow found comfort in such melancholy, at least they found comfort that such melancholy could be shared. The gripping moments that brought these two men together men left them spiritually displaced. There was a moment in each man's history filled with wild-eyed bewilderment, a moment that wrenched at the soul, hateful vibrations that could find no harmony no matter how long one looked. Thrilling and fearful moments left their mark. The thrill and the fear eternally branded them. They were left wide-eyed and white-knuckled, and were asked to function as blissful-innocents. James appeared to be an innocent victim to Ron, and James saw Ron as a victim likewise, just a bit less innocent. The fundamentals of their mentalities of life were very different, but their roads were destined to cross. They shared an honest, humble disposition, and something of a romance was in their stars for the duration of their short acquaintance. Ron ate his breakfast and the two walked to the lounge. CNN was on the television, and Ron began to talk to James.

"I've been in the Marines for twelve years now, and every time I watch the national news I get more and more disgusted with society."

"There *is* a bunch of greedy slime in this country, and the world for that matter. That's half the reason I'm in this place." James replied.

"You're right, but that's not exactly what I mean. The people who make the decisions don't see the dirty underbelly of their wake. I've gone to war for this country, and more and more it seems like it is a bunch of idiots who make all the decisions. I guess you're right in saying that they're greedy, but either way, that's not what I lay my life on the line for."

"You mean all the *professionals* are jaded? They have their heads up their ass?"

"Yeah, they all want their leather chairs and BMW's, but don't want to take a dime out of their pockets to give to the weak or the needy."

"So we have a bunch of slimy 'professionals' in this country?"

"Yeah. Yeah, you were right! You seem like a smart kid, James. How did you ever end up in this place?"

"I launched an 80 pound ceramic vat through the windshield of my dad's truck, then called the cops on myself."

Ron laughed to himself a little bit.

"You two don't get along?"

"No, we get along fine for the most part. He sent me off to work in a butcher shop in Montana when I turned eighteen. After spending five years covered in blood for 70 hours a week I couldn't take it anymore and came home. My youth was a bit short-changed. That's all I have against my dad, but there was just something about that truck. It just seemed to wreak of evil. It was something intangible that threw me over the top."

"I hear you man. When I came back from war I had PTSD. It took me a few years to get back to normal. I still have night terrors like I dream that I am still in a hot zone. Sometimes it's war-like dreams, but sometimes it's spiritual. I wake up at night and it takes me a minute before I calm down."

The two passed the day talking about the uglier aspects of life, and the solace of death. There is a bit of comfort that one faces at the end of their life knowing that they no longer have to suffer the vices of this mortal world. The realization of one's devices pains the soul. Pain was common-ground for Ron and James. Pain puts pleasure into a frame of reference and makes pleasure something worth striving for. Pain is a product of the sacrifices made to produce luxury. We face cheats. We face greed. There is no free lunch, and nature always bats last. There is always a sacrifice required to produce luxury, and humans (and the world for that matter) are left in the balance. Those who see these sacrifices being made value resources differently. Their discretion of wind and water, people and time are seen through purer eyes. Their eyes cause them great pain, but they understand the meaning of the word harmony better than the blissfully ignorant. Whether or not they knew it, both Ron and James shared the thought "Who would I be without my pains?" Both men spent considerable time close to death. They both became callous to the idea of the end of mortal life, and spent many a pondering moment contemplating what lies beyond our mortal realm of existence. Both men welcomed the idea of passing on, but that is not to say that both men had any intention of floating through the rest of their life in somber satisfaction, physically, mentally, or spiritually. By most, death is viewed at as a gloomy pomp, a loss of vitality. For Ron and James death was the freedom to transcend from mere mortals into the great spirits that these warriors have shaped their souls into. Ron had already fought all of his battles, but James was only afoot of his. All the time spent as a witness of death made them both more comfortable with passing on, and less easy about living in the world that was built around them. Ron and James could grasp the concept of harmony. It was a world where sacrifices were proportional to the rewards. Unfortunately everyone wanted something they could hold on to, and furthermore as more was received, more was desired. Nothing was proportional. Not war, not the slaughter house, and not the Seventh Floor. Ron and James were forced into an uncomfortable reality. They were mere cogs in the mean machine that is society, and they felt trapped by the greed that surrounded them. Ron was 'coming back to reality' as his road in life crossed James', but

James couldn't tell if he was coming closer to death, or getting further away from it.

As the two sat together Ron noticed a look of peace smeared across James face. He looked at the boy with admiration. He could see that something burned bright and hot inside of James. That image gave Ron hope. He saw a boy who was learning who he was. Ron believed he saw a boy who had figured out life, and faith, and happiness. Ron believed he saw a young man who had decided to hold closest to his heart the things that no one could take away. James was working on building a new heaven as he laid in this prison, this hell. Nothing important had pertinent, declared ownership. No, those things were all intangible, and no one could stake claim to them. Nirvana? James was there. Aside from Ron, everyone was puzzled and even a little uneasy about the look on James's face. It was a look that had been frozen on his face for three days now. James finally detached himself from the evils that haunted him on the outside world. He walked away from the slaughter house in Montana, and into the Seventh Floor. He fled one tyrant just to land in the hands of another, but he no longer struggled for control in his life. He let go and let God make all the hard decisions for him. True, James was confined to the walls of the Seventh Floor, but he accepted nothing they had to offer, not the food, and certainly not the psychological authority. This place was no less hectic, or depraved of reason than the outside world, and furthermore, James couldn't have appeared more out of place from the mayhem that existed on the slimy underbelly of the Seventh Floor. Some of the professionals saw the tranquility in James as progress, but not Dr. Chode. He saw it as defeat. James became keen to the game Chode was playing. In spite of his failure,

Dr. Chode craved dissecting James's psychology, and twisting and mashing it until James cried for mercy. No knew what to truly make of the unearthly, peaceful aura James carried.

Chapter 13

(fifth day of fasting)

James's 15th day began with a peculiar question from Ron.

"Last night I slept the whole way through the night. That's the first time in years that I've been able to do that, but I had the strangest dream. It was you, floating above a grassy knoll wearing a full Indian headdress, and when I woke up this morning I couldn't get the words Sweet Grass Hill out of my head. Does any of that mean anything to you?"

James was baffled. He couldn't help but think of Coyote. It was a sign that something big was brewing, and it was the best validation he had thus far in connection to the spirit world. James had his own exotic dreams, but another man's dreams depicting scenes from his vision quest, the intangible things like how he felt after the peyote began to take effect baffled James. He didn't know how to respond. Part of him wanted to cry out "Yes, I will be the great warrior of my people!" but James didn't want to come off as psychotic, so he took his time and replied with reservation.

"Yeah I've been to Sweet Grass Hill."

"What about the Indian headdress? What do you think it means?" Ron continued to question.

"Look man, there's some things I don't want to talk about, at least not here and now. Ya dig?"

"I feel ya man. I'll let it go, but in my dream you had this aura about you that seemed so pure, and unified with everything that's good. I have things I don't want to talk about, but those things aren't as pure and godly as the way I dreamed of you."

"Maybe I wasn't the man in your dreams." James rebutted.

"No, it was you."

James avoided Ron for the rest of the day. Ron's dream rattled James, and James spent the rest of the day trying to collect himself. His fasting began pushing new levels of euphoria, but he started to lose that inner peace he had just a day before. He started seeing portals at the end of hallways. Bright figures glowed from the edges of windows and dark figures crept and lurched in intimidation in the shadows. Spirits were crossing over and James was only getting a glimpse of them, but it was enough to shatter any man's conception of reality. James began to get the feeling that strange things were about to happen.

Positive and negative energy continued to come and go in cycles, but the amplitude of each episode was beginning to push James into places he had never been before. He never conceived the full magnitude of the spirit world. He had only a taste, and it appetized him. James began to think he may have bitten off more than he could chew. He didn't know what to make of it. It was hard to maintain and find balance. He knew erratic behavior would soon follow if he didn't make the next move. He had to get a grip on things, and returning to eating seemed like a viable path. But James vowed on his soul that he would die locked up on the

Seventh Floor before he would eat another morsel of food in front of that glutton, Dr. Chode. The whole idea of a stranger envisioning him in such a way pushed James beyond the threshold of his comfort level. He was once again knee deep in the uneasy mayhem of the Seventh Floor trying to make basic social and societal connections. He paced the halls until craft-time. James walked into the craft room, and noticed a drawing one of the patients was working on. It was a picture of hearts dripping from the leaves of trees. The positive energy was flowing, but maybe just a bit too heavy for James. He took a couple of deep breaths, then pulled up a seat next to Chuck. Chuck was an old-timer who had been on the Seventh Floor since about the time James started fasting.

James asked Chuck a question, as heavy a question as one man could ask another in that situation. Neither man possessed the mental qualities that define a sane individual.

"Chuck, what do you see when you look into my eyes."

"I see a young man with grey eyes searching for beauty, but your heart, your heart is fit for war."

War was not what James was in search of when he launched that ceramic vat through the window of the big, red Dodge. Chuck's words sent James staggering in fear. The uneasy feeling of the slaughter house re-developed in the pit of James's stomach, and multiplied. He was just a boy who was asked to be more of a man than anyone he had ever met. There was no comfort in the truth. When James opened his eyes to the supernatural reality around him, Coyote's prophecy was becoming more and more explicit. Ron, Chuck, and the Seventh Floor were hinting towards the duty James would be asked to fulfill. He had wrapped himself in the prophecy on such a superficial level that he believed himself to be noble and righteous, but he had yet to do anything noble or righteous, and as prophecy of his great battle was about to be fulfilled, James seemed to be lacking the courage he needed. James started to forget the game with Dr. Chode and walked back to his room and began to pray.

"Jehovah, you are Apistotoke, creator. Jehovah, you ar Naato'si, sun god. Jehovah, you are Ko'kimiki'somma, moon god. Jehovah, bless me with the strength to fight this battle. I know not my enemy, but it is evil. Jehovah, give me strength."

Dr. Chode was listening to James with an ear against the closed door. When it sounded like James was done praying, Dr. Chode skulked away. He had James pinned. Dr. Chode had no idea what James was saying or praying about, but it sounded crazy enough to Dr. Chode to put James in the funny farm.

James continued to pray. "God, I know not my adversary. Give me the knowledge to know who I am fighting. Give me the strength to be your great warrior."

Those simple prayers brought peace to James as he sat in his room and meditated for the rest of the day. He cleared his mind of all his fears. He rationalized his whole situation. The worst thing that could happen to him was death. He had spent so many hours so close to death, that it had no intimidation over him. He feared not the things he could not explain. He humbled himself and thought, "I am only a man, and there is much my mind cannot grasp." The strange and eerie sights and feelings, he had dissolved. All the lies and fallacies of the Seventh Floor fell beneath him. Dr. Chode's game, and the opinion of all the professionals meant nothing to James. The psychotic realities of all the patients were lost in the periphery. James transcended through everything. He passed through Nirvana and as that supreme state of peace left him, he felt strength begin to burn inside of him. It was strong but gentle, and built faith in himself. He was beginning to believe he could conquer whatever demons laid before him. The feeling James had inside of him was divine and reached out beyond our mortal dimension calling forth all sorts of spirits. They came and watched over James and began to see the transformation from a young man into a spiritual warrior.

The day passed and night fell. Ron and James went to sleep once again and when they woke in the morning Ron once again confronted James.

"I had another dream last night."

James's gut tightened as he gathered the strength to face whatever symbolic insight Ron was about to bestow on James.

"Let's hear it," James bravely requested.

"Well, at first you were sitting in a dull green room. It looked like you were sleeping, but you were upright. You had the most pleasant smile on your face, and your breathing and heart beat took a calm rhythm that seemed to last all night. After what seemed like an eternity, you slowly opened your eyes, and your stomach turned translucent. You could see a small flame in your belly. Then, you took a couple strands of twine, but this was no ordinary twine. It was alive. It pulsated with a rhythm and you sat awake and braided a rope out of this twine. As you braided, the twine pulsated harder and harder, and the fire in your belly grew bigger and brighter, and the walls of the dull green room began to turn into technicolor fractals and melted away into nothing. Do you think it means anything?"

"Maybe I'm getting stronger. Who's to say any dream really has a definitive meaning. You, of all people, should understand that."

"Yeah, I understand, but these dreams are so vivid, and *you* are the main character. It just has me puzzled. I never had dreams like this. I mean I never had *good* dreams like this, and never about people I hardly even know."

James spent the rest of the day braiding his rope. He sat in his room in complete silence. The room was dark, and the only light was coming from the sun shining through the small double-paned windows. As he sat in meditation, his breathing was calm and steady, and opened his eyes on occasion. He felt a utopian glory, where everyone made the sacrifices to sustain themselves. Glory filled his soul. Reward was proportional, and harmony was present. The cycles of positive and negative energy mellowed just enough for James to match their magnitude. After a few hours he began speaking in tongues. Luckily Dr. Chode had already made his rounds for the day, and never witnessed this. As the Holy Spirit moved through James and he spoke gently, he felt energy pulsate, starting in his chest and belly, moving through his arms and legs and out to his fingers and toes.

The energy spilt from his fingertips and cast a translucent shimmering light into the room. It rippled through the air and chased away the darkness, making it shiver in fear. It smelled pleasant, and spoke with a deep angelic voice. It was comforting to every neuron in the body. James opened his eyes once again, and began to see the power that came from within him. He felt confident in himself as the Holy Spirit fill James and spewed out from his limbs. What he saw before him validated what he was lead to believe all this time. In all the privation of the Seventh Floor James cultivated a spiritual essence that was capable of greatness. All uncertainty was gone. All his Earthly desires left him, and James knew he was ready for whatever battle laid ahead.

Over the next five days James was able to understand and embrace the waves of positive energy, and fearlessly face the waves of negative energy. It took time to become familiar with the supernatural, and furthermore James was the only man capable of such growth. The spirit within him fed on every morsel of positive energy that flowed through his prison. The rhythm of the day continued into the night, and James became the epicenter of all the vibrations. Energy brewed within him, and expelled without. All life fed from it and took notice in his direction. The negative energy was brewing, and that too took notice in his direction.

Chapter 14

(eleventh day of fasting)

On the morning of the 21st day of his stay on the Seventh Floor James was confronted by Ron once again. Ron had a bit of a sullen look on his face when he sat down to talk with James.

"I had another dream about you last night," he said a bit uneasily. "I dreamt you were in the desert hunting. You weren't hunting game though. You were hunting the Devil."

James took it lightly.

"Ron, I've been hunting demons for as long as I can remember. Maybe I'll catch him. Wouldn't that be something!" laughed James.

James's humor didn't bring any comfort to Ron. He just began to tense up inside. It took him back to the frame of mind he lived in while he was in combat. It was a frame of mind that welcomed adversity and aggression. It was a frame of a mind on the prowl. What was so staggering to Ron, though, was how the spirits of good and evil seemed so definitive before James. Good and evil were always real to Ron. He always believed in a higher power, and existence beyond our realm, but the vivid ideas of good and evil in his dreams were built around obscure principles. Who was James? Why is the spirit flowing so strongly in this demented location? Nothing made good sense to Ron, but he couldn't help but feel the crushing weight that James was feeling at the same time. If he only knew what James knew, maybe he would be more at ease. Ron couldn't take the tension of his dreams anymore. His dreams were as gripping as the presence of James before him. Both seemed to be stitched together with a hint of psychedelic euphoria. The cyclical patterns of positive and negative energy weighed on Ron just as they did James. Ron never asked for this, and much less expected such an experience in the mental ward of Good Samaritan Hospital. He was simply conditioned to feel such energies. All that time spent at war heightened his awareness towards the energy of good and evil. He could feel wavelengths and frequencies that only he and James could sense. Whatever Ron felt in the presence and at the thought of James was too raw to be a psychotic delusion. He distanced himself from James for the rest of his stay on the Seventh Floor.

Ron came to the Seventh Floor trying to solve a problem, a mental issue, and it only got worse. It's a lot like when you put an animal in a cage. Their emotions build and build until they boil over. Deprivation from justice and commonplace is no cure for any illness, especially psychological ones. The brain must be at peace. It cannot be starved of the exercise and function of compassion and humanity. When the brain is deprived of commonplace, your scope of reality begins to get twisted as you have no proper frame of reference. Only the soul and spirit within a man can fight to preserve what he knows is right. Sometimes that means detaching yourself from all of your Earthly needs. James did just that, but Ron seemed to be an innocent by standard, blindsided by James's spiritual journey upon the Seventh Floor. Ron's final dream began to spark emotions of bewilderment, emotions that he worked so hard to detach himself from when he came home from battle. It was that wild-eyed feeling that both Ron and James fought against to achieve the inner peace they so desired.

For James that inner peace was imperative. He knew not the particulars of his ultimate purpose, but from what he gathered from every acquaintance made, he could not possibly succeed as a warrior if he remained bound by any Earthly desire. He gave up on validation from Dr. Chode, or any of the professionals. He gave up on freedom from the Seventh Floor, because he had transcended everything they tried to pin him down with. Those physical hells of battle in our realm are so driven by rage-filled emotions, emotions that grip the spinal column and twist out from the senses anything that is familiar and comfortable. All that is left is detached, empty mania. Emotions are what make any animal dangerous, but James did not need to be dangerous. He needed to be powerful, and that is staked in whole by a combination of knowledge and patience. A man who is slow to anger is more powerful than the mighty. Moving beyond the grip of emotions marks the highest degree of mental strength. You must know your strengths and weaknesses as well as your adversary's strengths and weaknesses. Knowledge is power. Furthermore, power comes in the patience of looking past all your emotions of wild-eyed bewilderment and executing calculated reactions. The state of mind James had achieved up to this point was no small feat. He detached himself from all his Earthly fears of privation by depriving himself one of the most integral ingredients in sustaining human life: food. He fasted and it elevated his state of mind until he felt connected with every great spirit known to man throughout the history of humanity. He put faith in those spirits, and it was faith alone, faith in himself and his God, that prepared him to wage war upon the greatest evil he would ever face.

Chapter 15

(twelfth day of fasting)

The 22nd morning of James's stay on the Seventh Floor began strangely. James woke with a pounding head and a racing heart. He felt staggered in time and space, and it took him a few deep breaths before he could gather himself. He felt the blood circulate from his head back down through his limbs and body. Slowly, he rose out of bed. There was an eerie feeling in the air that was making the hair on the back of James's neck stand on end. He walked down to the end of the east wing while the rest of the ward was eating breakfast. James watch the sunrise, and the sky turn from orange to blue. He stayed there for a while and contemplated his existence. There was a hitch in the air that provoked a philosophical side in James. He separated the sensual from the transcendental. Then once they were isolated, he unified them. He decided only two forces composed our realm: Consciousness and energy. James thought about the fundamentals that made him who he came to be. He walked the timeline of his life from a young child, to a young man, to being a patient on the Seventh Floor. He thought about how specialized his thought process had become as he began to get more and more detached from all the fundamentals of what the average citizen calls reality. It was the first time in a few weeks that James began to think about these things, and as he did he began to feel depressed. How long would he wait for this great battle if it was not the one being played out against Dr. Chode? James could feel the bile in his gut begin to back up into his stomach and thought this would be a good place to end it. He turned about face and walked back down the hall. As he passed the nurses' desk he met the acquaintance of a treacherous grin clothed in a black silk suit.

"I am Silas. How do you do?"

The sight and sound of Silas curdled James' empty belly. James could smell a strong desire for the sensual life on Silas's breath. It was thick and harsh like garlic flavored kerosene. The energy that Silas gave off seemed to creep and lurch in time with the Seventh Floor. It was sleazy. Silas was sleazy. His presence sent off a jolt that disrupted natural harmony in the mind, body, and spirit. He had the same condescending stance as all professionals. James would have never guessed the man to be a patient, but he heard the nurses gabbing about him, and James soon concluded the improbable to be truth in the flesh. Silas landed on the Seventh Floor after being picked up by the police. No one knew exactly where he was from, but the authorities had their eyes on him for a few months. He had been hopping from town to town, city to city, preaching how he was the second coming of Christ. He had the persona of Charles Manson, and as he preached with great grandeur, a clear, colorless liquid oozed through the airwaves making all who listened drunk with greed and lust. As James walked away, he could hear Silas talking to a young, attractive, female patient

"We need more women like you in this world. God intended us to live lives of pleasure, and you look like you could supply a supple supplement of that. Don't listen to the people in here. You have a gift, but if you listen to these people you will never put it to good use."

Silas was no dummy. He knew how to get what he wanted out of people. He wanted everything. He wanted every luxury sewn from another man's back and wanted everyone on Earth to desire the same thing. He made no effort himself. He never toiled or labored. He hardly knew what activity was, but any challenge to the man's self-worth, and he made no reservations in cutting a man down as low as he could take them. Everything that was righteous in Silas's eyes was a means of immediate gratification. Sex, money, drugs, lavish meals were the only purpose to live. The higher pleasures in life, anything ethical, was meaningless to Silas. His message was simple. His message was not a simple life. It was to live for whatever brought pleasure in the moment. That all sounded very attractive to everyone he ever spoke with, but Silas could care less about the quality of life his message delivered. He had a different motive. He had no desire to truly sustain the good in the world. He wanted a world of cripples. He wanted a world that feared any privation from indulgence.

Silas' message was convincing, but it lacked any virtue that could define it as righteous and holy. The authorities didn't like him, but he didn't break any laws until he arrived at James' town and began his cunning deliverance of women, forming a cult that had the smell and stature of a prostitution ring. Silas was like a combination of Jim Jones and Charles Manson. James began to get angry and irritated as he listened to the conversation behind his back. He took a look over his shoulder, and saw Silas whisper something into the young girl's ear. James watched the man's lips move with a devilish look in his eye. His sly eyelids tensed. They cut right through the girl down to her soul. Silas seemed to see the weakness in her mind and spirit. He spoke his words with a velvety tongue. When they landed at their destination they seemed to sooth and intrigue the girl all in the same moment. The whole sequence of events burrowed deep in James' skin. It antagonized him. He could hardly bear it to see such a devil play with the minds of such innocent people. He was as repulsive as Dr. Chode.

Silas delivered his slimy message with so much class and grandeur that the authorities thought the Seventh Floor was the only reasonable place for the man until any definite decisions could be made of his fate. He flapped his lips with peeled eyes as his brow wriggled and contorted like a snake. He moved with so much splendor, that he was disgusting to every nerve in James' body. He moved his hands, arched his back, and stuck out his chest as if to say "I am the classiest man who ever lived." Silas presented himself without any degree of couth or comfortable level of body language. He was the embodiment of everything that James found vile in society. He preached his message of wealth and pleasure without ever batting an eye at the sacrifices made to achieve such luxuries. James began to feel the rage and hate he felt in the slaughter house. To James, Silas was the slime that infected everything right and good in the world. He was the Bastard that spread the myth of greed and personal gain. Every sound that came out of his mouth was pompous to the point that the listener couldn't even think for themselves. He took a deep breath before he spoke, and as he spoke his words with a self-absorbed tone, dragging every syllable, declaring, "Every man is weak. He should find his strength in a strong, sexy woman." He was a paralyzing parasite that burrowed a cavity in the mind of everyone he met and made them believe in the malicious fallacies of evil and corruption. He could tell you everything you wanted to hear, and could bring substance to his myths. James was transcending deep into the spirit world by this point in his fast, and he could sense something about Silas.

James could sense a supernatural power within Silas. All the persuasion in Silas' voice, and the fruition in his movements struck nerves in James that he didn't know existed. James could feel something about Silas that was demonic. He was intelligent and at least as dangerous as any man who may have walked the Earth before him. Naturally, he and Dr. Chode got along famously, but he was not to be released until a proper assessment had been made. Silas separated and elevated himself from the rest of the patients on the Seventh Floor. Free or detained, Silas was out to make a point, and let his presence be known. His disposition was so self-righteous and self-indulged that anyone with any degree of innocence and clarity could see right through the bullshit. For the first time in his 22 days on the Seventh Floor, James was in the company of person at least as repulsive as Dr. Chode, and that man was Silas.

Lunch call came and James sat in the cafeteria with a book in hand, 12 days into his fast. Silas picked up his tray and spotted James from across the room sitting by himself. He walked over and sat down opposite James.

"I don't believe I caught your name this morning when I said hello."

"My name is James," he replied, disinterestedly.

"Well James, you look like a lonely soul, and I don't see a plate in front of you. May I ask why?"

"I'm fasting." He said

"Well that's a fabulous waste of effort if you ask me. Like this hamburger for example, enjoying such a thing is what pleases God, don't you know. It's not caviar, but it's so succulent. To think, such a beast gave up its life to please my appetite, is wholly satisfying. I like tasting all the juices. That lets you know it was a living, breathing creature at one time."

"What I crave is intangible, a higher level of consciousness. Did it ever cross your mind that the greatest gifts God gives are those things that cannot be held, or in your case, tasted?"

"You might be on to something James. What do you say you and I should be friends, pal?"

"I don't like you. I don't like the way you look. I don't like the way you smell. I don't like the way you walk, talk, or treat people, and I really don't like your opinion on life. So, well dude... count me out."

James turned his attention to his book and remained in his seat. He'd be damned if he let Silas get the best of him. Instead, James sat there coolly until Silas became so uncomfortable that *he* was the one who got up and left. It was a simple exercise in psychology. James wasn't about to let a vicious man like Silas get the upper hand in their relationship. James could have easily gotten up and walked away and shown Silas how much he disliked him, but instead James sat there until Silas developed a subliminal fear of James. James set the tone when he gave no ground. He had been playing this game with Dr. Chode for weeks. Now Silas was the primary antagonist intersecting James' road. Silas was just another patient, but he wasn't *just another patient.* Silas lacked that element of ignorance that qualified so many of the patients on the Seventh Floor as innocent. He was a well-educated man, or at least appeared that way. He was too smart to be casually ignored, and he was a bit too obnoxious to be easily ignored. He was a thorn in James' side. But, the three weeks James' had spent on the Seventh Floor had conditioned him to strive beyond all instigation Silas brought forth, and maintain inner peace and quiet control of the power struggle that was beginning to brew between the two men.

Night fell, and James slept uncomfortably through the night with demonic nightmares. He saw himself locked in a small room with a dim flickering light, and a voice hissed over the intercom. It spiked the nerves with a deep desire to strike fear in the man, but James never broke down and cried for help. The whole way through his dream, he stood tall, and found comfort from within. The fear of mortality had been surpassed through his fast, and he knew his soul was safe with the Lord. Temptation was the only pit-fall that James could have fallen to. There was nothing tempting about his dream though. It was shear wrath, pride, and intimidation. James eased into the discomfort and rode his inner-peace all the way into the morning. He woke before sunrise, drenched in sweat. He crawled out of bed and walked down to the lavatory, and took a cold shower. He focused on the chill that penetrated his skin and let it soak in deep until he began to shiver, then turned off the water, grabbed his towel, dried off and got dressed. He walked down to the lounge and turned on the television.

James was beginning to understand just what he was supposed to fight. It was everything that Silas preached. James began to believe that he was to save his fellow patients upon the Seventh Floor. The critique and criticism of Dr. Chode coupled with the deceptions of vice delivered by Silas brewed a matrix of evil that James felt compelled to stand up against. He had the right set of eyes to see the fall of the Seventh Floor before it happened. Ron couldn't help him with this one. James was on his own.

The patients were called to breakfast, and to James' surprise, Silas walked into the room and sat down next to him.

"I have a little something for you since you're fasting," Silas said, as he pulled out a can of snuff. "I know how much you like it," he said with a devilish grin. James thought back to the many nights he sat out on Sweet Grass Hill fireside with a rip of tobacco between his lip and gum. James wondered how this man knew such things about him. Suspicion filled James as he began to suspect the worst.

"I don't think you know me well enough to understand what I like and dislike" James said, "but I know exactly what you are up to." James rebutted.

"You know me? Ha! I have smoked the finest opium in the East. I have drunk the boldest coffee of Arabia. I have tasted the lust in Amsterdam. I have bathed in the greed of Las Vegas." He seethed. "I am Silas, the Anti-Christ!"

Chapter 16

(thirteenth day of fasting)

Upon Silas's final interjection of haste, James was ripped from his realm and the reality of the Seventh Floor, and was spat into the spirit world. James found himself in a cave. The air was cold and dank, and there was no light. Chills ran up and down his spine. He could see nothing as he strained his sight in the darkness. He could hear water slowly drip as the eeriest voice pierced through the blind darkness.

"I am Silas. You know no pain like the pain I inflict. You will feel it. There is a way that I will shed my mercy upon you. Denounce your God and I will light your cell and deliver you to that despicable comfort you call home," Silas cried through the darkness. His voice was the most discomforting hiss. It penetrated with a bitter bite more ferocious than the frigid air. It reached down into James' soul and shook with all the evil Silas could muster, but James was not rattled. The voice that hissed in that cave would have bewildered any man not as spiritually mature as James, but he dug deep for peace in his soul which he honed under the paw of Dr. Chode while on the Seventh Floor. James believed deep down inside that good would always prevail. He began to grin as he remembered an old Townes Van Zandt song that played on the radio in the butcher shop and brought a little peace and courage to him. James began to sing. "Salvation sat and crossed herself, called the devil partner. Wisdom burned upon a shelf, who'll kill the raging cancer. Seal the river at its mouth, take the water prisoner. Fill the sky with screams and cries, bath in fiery answer." As James sang, a technicolored light began to shine from below like in Ron's dream when James was braiding his rope. James followed the light, leading him out of the cave and into the star-lit desert. He was stunned with amazement as he walked beneath the vast expanse of stars. A twinkling constellation caught his eye. It was Scorpio. Scorpio began to talk to James, and asked him if they could wander the sky again like that night on Sweet Grass Hill. James said he couldn't and began to explain to Scorpio that he was hunting evil. Scorpio understood and wished to give James a blessing. He asked if James would only close his eyes for a second. James thought it was a small request for something such as Scorpio's blessing. James closed his eyes, then opened them. When he opened his eyes he was stunned with what he was seeing. Scorpio had blessed him to be the fiercest hunter in all the desert. Scorpio had turned James into a 6 foot long Scorpion with a sleek black exoskeleton and the gnarliest of a stinger and pinchers. They were barbed and serrated, grizzly to boot and hard as diamonds. James was delighted, and the joy within him began to bubble, but he was sure not to let his emotions get the best of him. He knew he had to remain sharp.

Silas was out there, and James didn't have the slightest idea where to look. As he glanced at the horizon he saw a vast expanse of sand and rock, canyons and buttes, populated by the occasional assembly of dead brush, dried flowers, and cacti. Every piece of the desert seemed to turn and take notice to James once he had Scorpio's blessing. There was a reverence. James understood his objective with a divine level of clarity. He had learned a lot about himself on the Seventh Floor and remembered from his experiences that the virtue of humility had worth far beyond its face value. Though he was strong, he was careful not to let his ego get the best of him. He needed to be focused, not proud. Too easily, a man fails to execute in full effect when pride and ego fills the soul. James walked slowly, humbly, and began to search for anything that might lead him to Silas. The spirit world was foreign to James. It was a place where the sights and sounds were unfamiliar and followed few laws of nature, but the feelings the atmosphere derived made perfect sense. The spirit that James captured on Sweet Grass Hill and on the Seventh Floor were embodied in every object found in that dark desert landscape. It was vast and begged of you to find direction from within. There was no assistance, no supplement of energy. It heightened the senses, and extruded the will. With every step the soul looked long and hard at all its flaws and all its beauties. With every step the sand crunched like crusted snow under James's legs as he cruised along the desert. The air smelled sweet like a musk of sage and citrus. Most of the plants were hiding behind a mask of dead bark. They knew evil was afoot, but shivered with joy as James cruised past as all the lives disguised in their detritus husk. James was looking for anything that sent the same feeling as the slaughter house rushing through his viens. He was looking for that same feeling he had when Silas first spoke to him on the Seventh Floor. James was hunting anything that gave him that blood-curdling, evil feel.

As James was cruising the desert, he noticed a cactus down on its knees praying. James thought this to be a bit peculiar, so he began to talk to the cactus.

"May I ask what you are doing?" James pried

"I am praying. See, a very evil creature has come to find haven in our desert. I am praying that God will send a warrior to save us." The cactus replied.

"I believe I am the warrior God has sent to save your desert. I am here to find the Antichrist and send him back to Hell."

"Well, you are a rather large scorpion. I was told Star Boy would come to our salvation. What makes you divine?"

"Years ago, I had a vision quest on Sweet Grass Hill, and I was told that I would be a great warrior. Recently I was locked up on the Seventh Floor of a mental hospital and have been fasting for the past 13 days. I am here to defeat the Antichrist, but I need help. I don't know where to find him."

"I'll help you!" the Cactus cried. "This Antichrist you speak of must be the Great Horned Snake and I will help you find him!"

Cactus got up, and the two began walking through the dark desert. The winds kicked up and began blowing sand in their faces. It yipped and howled like the voice of Coyote but the two were determined to find signs that would lead them to the Great Horned Snake, Silas, the Anti-Christ.

"The last time it was night time in the desert, Sage was kidnapped. His sweet perfume no longer filled the air. He returned when the sun rose, but I am not sure if he will be safe tonight," Cactus said in a worried meter.

The thought of Star Boy saving his people ruminated in James' mind. He looked to the skies, and found direction in the stars. He felt the ebb and flow of their energy as they shined down on the spirit world. The cycles of time and energy swayed hither, and thither, and yon'. The eerie feeling of the cave shifted into something positive by the time James began to talk to Cactus. Time seemed to be standing still in those intimidating moments, but sped to warp-speed during the comfortable ones. It all inspired thoughts in James' mind; he had not eaten in 13 days. He prayed something silently, and embraced Cactus in his prayer. He also began to understand the soul of the desert was not unified. There were breaks and hummocks, patches of negativity, and patches of positive energy.

"It has been day in the desert for a very long time, at least five years, but recently the sun has begun to set, and now it is night. Night is not good in the desert for my friends and I. Evil seems to grow, and the beauty of the desert hides. The only good that remains are the stars."

James looked at the stars and thought for a moment.

"If only I could see what the stars see." Then with a bit of haste he turned to Cactus. "Can you show me where Sparrow lives?" He asked

"Sparrow lives with my brothers. They are not far away," Cactus replied.

The two of them began walking towards where the Cactus' brothers lived. As they ventured closer to the location, minerals appeared in the sand. They were glowing brighter in shades of blue, green, pink and purple. The wind kept yipping and howling, but the scent of Sage was no longer detectable to the nose. Cactus grew nervous, and with good reason. When they arrived they found Sparrow along with some disheartening news. All of Cactus's brothers were dead.

"How could this happen?" They asked Sparrow.

"A great vulture came down from the sky and tore them apart." Sparrow replied. "I was fast enough to escape."

Cactus wept. "My brothers were so harmless," he thought. "How could anyone do such a thing." Cacti bring so much life and beauty to the desert. Whoever or whatever did this wanted to destroy something beautiful. Cactus' emotions went from the very top to the very bottom. His peaceful desert was under attack, and Silas was at the root of it. All the beauty and splendor of the spring-desert turned into the vast, desolate winter. Cactus turned to James and said,

"I cannot go on. I must stay and mourn my brothers' death."

James understood, but gained determination afoot of the immediate tragedy. James wondered "If I was Silas, the Great Horned Snake, where would I hide?" He had a thought, and turned and asked Sparrow if he could climb on his back, and fly high in the sky, and search for a place the Great Horned Snake might hide. Sparrow took off, beating his wings with such haste that he began to sweat in the cold night desert. He flew in a circle, then a bigger circle, then in a bigger circle. James soon began to smell the scent of blood and raw meat. Adrenaline surged through his veins. His exoskeleton began to tighten as he spotted a canyon of black rocks stained with red streaks, and he could hear a creature taking long, heavy breaths.

James was beginning to feel out the sensations derived from the exoskeleton he acquired from Scorpio. It was strange. So exact, and rigid. It was cold. There was none of the comforting insulation offered by the fat found in mammals. Sparrow landed, and James crawled off of his back. When his legs hit the sand all time was lost, and James felt a sense of clarity that was beyond anything he had ever experienced before. He felt space oscillate in cycles. As he embraced those cycles, the rhythm of the spirit world became apparent, and James moved in harmony with it. As he did, he began to see the energy and consciousness of all that dwelled in that place, as well as their fears and affinities. Sparrow bid James farewell and James set out to fulfill prophecy. As he lumbered along, the moon began to speak to him in a voice so soft it could barely be heard. She said be brave and believe in yourself. The feeling of battle became eminent. He cruised the desert towards the canyon, and the glow from the minerals in the sands grew dimmer and dimmer. James was so focused. Nothing could remove him from that precise point in his mind, even though Silas picked the perfect battle ground. The desert can be so vast that the mind begins to wander as all the references between space and time vanish. In the spring time when all the plants are in bloom there is no place more beautiful and livelier than the desert. All the plants and flowers give definition to beauty, and belonging, but spring had turned to winter in the blink of an eye, and all that beauty turned to lifelessness. Now, only snakes and scorpions roamed the desert. No flowers swimming in the oases. No cacti chasing each other over the sand. No festivals of life where the plants and animals danced full of life to the rhythm of the day. No, this was a place where the most confident of spirits began to question themselves in the hunt for evil.

Reason and rationale seem to disappear with the vegetation as the seasons change and life leaves. James was once again on a journey in his mind, alone with himself, and in the danger of introspective doubt. James kept lumbering along looking for the canyon, all the while Moon whispering comforting words in his ear. A pungent musk spread throughout the air that made eyes tear up and stomachs turn. As James continued on the hunt, he began to understand exactly what that smell was. It was fear. The stench fueled the fire inside of James like the scent of blood to a predator. He became eager, and the adrenaline flowed. He was careful not to get excited. Precision and clarity could have been so easily lost to the impulses of excitement, but fortunately for James he had not gotten excited about anything since that professional told him he was not fit to be released. He had to be keen, make calculated decisions, and take calculated actions. Silas may have been giving off the scent of fear, but most creatures are most dangerous when their livelihood is being threatened.

James continued along the vast desert passing gatherings of lifeless husks of plants, and focusing on each step he took, understanding that each took him closer to Silas. He continued on, gaining in zeal as he closed the distance between himself and Silas. Finally James came to that canyon; a gnarly scar gouged into the black desert bedrock stained with red streaks. The smell of fear was thick as it floated through the air. The sky looked ominous. There were few stars and nearly no light. The red streaks oozed and dripped from overhead, viscous with a greasy sheen. Heavy breathing could be heard echoing down the canyon. James knew that this was the canyon where the Great Horned Snake, Silas, was hiding. Dark whispering cries hissed as James gazed deep into the crevasse. Such sounds would send chills down the spine of a lesser man, but James spent prisoned hours preparing his soul for the act he was about to execute.

He began walking up the canyon. He was getting nearer to Silas when thunder crashed and lightning broke from the sky, dumping torrents of rain into the desert. All the surface water hit the canyon and rushed downhill towards James like a thousand horses. The wall of water struck him with fury, and hauled him down the canyon with the water screaming like demons as it carried James back down to the mouth of the Canyon. For the first time in his life James felt fear for his mortality. The fear of one's own mortality is quite possibly the most genuine, eye-opening emotion a person can have. It sends you on an introspective journey that questions every morsel of your character. When you escape death you become more self-aware. You see the strength within you, and lose all sympathy for the devil. Everything seems so much purer and fundamental. Truth, reason, and purpose lie naked in front of you, and after James' little brush with death in the canyon, he snatched up all of this as easily as plucking leaves from a twig. He brushed himself off and scurried his six foot exoskeleton headlong up the canyon once more. As he did, a fire inside of him physically burned, and Ron's dream began to come to life. It started as a mild, tender flicker down in his belly, and grew stronger as he headed up the canyon. On his second trip up that scar cut into the breast of the desert, he heard the most demonic voice ever hissing tongues. The sounds slithered through the air, and pierced James's thoughts, but James continued towards his destination, unintimidated. As he cruised along he could see thousands of blood red spiders creeping back into the cracks of the cliffs as he approached. By the time James reached the head of the canyon the fire inside of him was now a roaring blaze. Smoked rolled out of his nostrils, and fire spat from his pinchers and stinger. At the head of the canyon James found a cave. He yelled into the cave

"Silas, come out and meet your fate!"

The hissing tongues were getting more demonic and more complex. At James' request, the Great Horned Snake slithered out from behind the rubble at the mouth of the cave. He was twenty feet long and as big around as a car tire. He moved slowly and flicked his yellow tongue and glared his yellow eyes. He hissed tongues at James.

"You in your filth, you think you are more virtuous than I? You know nothing of righteousness. I please a god far more than you ever will, or could even dream of."

"That will be a little hard when you're dead." James replied.

They charged at each other. As they did, swarms of hornets flew from Silas' eyes, and sulfur dripped from his fangs. His scaly hide stood erect with bards, as he slithered with the quickness of lightning. James thundered ahead, surviving the swarms of hornets. They attacked with ferocity, but could not break the shell of his exoskeleton with their stingers. And when he reached Silas in that scar gouged deep into the desert he was sure to be the first to strike. He snatched up Silas by the throat with his fiery pinchers, and drove his stinger deep into the head of the Great Horned Snake, injecting a healthy dose of Holy Water. Silas fell limp and lied dead on the cold desert ground in the cold desert night.

Chapter 17

James caught himself in a whirl-wind as the sun began to rise upon the spirit world. James could see Coyote on the horizon looking at back at him, smiling like a butcher's dog. At the blink of an eye he found himself sitting in the lounge of the Seventh Floor. Silas was lying in front of him with blood pouring out of his ears, eyes, mouth, and nose. James couldn't believe what he was seeing. He had killed the Anti-Christ! Coyote's prophecy had come true! The sight of Silas lying there, dead, before him shocked James. Stunned, James ran for help. It wasn't the fact that Silas had died that scared James. It was the fact that he was the only witness to what had happened and there was no chance in Hell that James would tell a soul what truly went down. He feared accusations of assault and murder. He sprinted down the hall to the nurses' desk.

"Come quick! Its Silas!" James prompted.

Two nurses hurried back to the lounge with James, and there they saw Silas lying dead on the floor with blood dripping from his face. They checked his vitals and radioed for doctors. They were in a frenzy when they finally asked James what happened.

"I don't know I think he had a seizure or something. He just started bleeding and fell out of his chair." James replied.

Doctors came up and took the body away. The whole floor was buzzing with whispers and big eyes all day. There was no sign of assault, so James was confronted with little address, and down inside he was smiling from ear to ear. He had defeated the Anti-Christ! Dr. Chode could sense a giddy contentment about James after Silas had died. Dr. Chode came up to James in the most unprofessional manner and asked,

"Why do *you* seem so happy? A man is dead!"

James took a second, and looked out the window. He could see the wild flowers on the hillside smiling, bowing down before him. The plants were once again dancing to the rhythm of the day.

"I feel like I have defeated whatever evil was in me." James replied with deep sincerity

Dr. Chode didn't know what to say. Any warm blooded mammal with half a heart would have taken satisfaction with James' words, but it only brewed suspicion within Dr. Chode. He was about to put the boots to James.

The next morning James rose with a bit of pride in his heart. To James he saved humanity from whatever heathen was about to brainwash social order the world over, and he was ready to leave the Seventh Floor. James was ready to feel the grass and sand beneath his feet. James was ready to feel the sunshine down on his face. James was ready to be free when Dr. Chode walked into his room on the 24th day of his stay on the Seventh floor.

"Pack your bags. You're going to the funny farm!" was all Dr. Chode said, and he walked out.

James had enough. He beat the traumatized state of mind he developed from working in the slaughter house. He found Nirvana. He beat the Anti-Christ. All that he wanted was to be free, and at the very least he deserved it. He conquered evil after evil, but evil still lived in people, and he would never have the power to completely conquer that. James contemplated attempting to escape once again, but he had no faith in the possibility of success. James's ego was growing, but it wasn't that he was self-absorbed. In fact the opposite couldn't be more true. His entire spirit was diffused into every environment he ever came in contact with; his home in Appalachia, the slaughter house in Montana, Sweet Grass Hill, the Seventh Floor, and humanity as a whole was richer for James had been there.

In a fit of self-righteous pride, James went sprinting down the south wing of the Seventh Floor towards the window at the end of the hall. He was about to get the ultimate one-up on Dr. Chode. James went crashing through the window. All the plants on the hillside took notice and feared the worst. Thunder rolled, and lightening struck. Paahsaakii looked to the sky with a solemn face and reverence in his soul as James fell seven floors to what should have been his ultimate death. Rain poured from the sky for the first time in over a month, and the greenbrier, maples, cacti, and grass wore the face of James.

Made in the USA
Columbia, SC
20 November 2024